# Sharon Marie Provost

# Shadow's Gate

Sharon Marie Provost

No part of this book may be reproduced, or stored in a retrieval system, or transmitted in any form or by any means, electronic, mechanical, photocopying, recording, or otherwise, without the express written permission of the publisher.

Cover photos by Sharon Marie Provost
Front: Fox Boarding House, Chinese Camp, California
Back: Solinsky Alley, Chinese Camp, California
Cover and interior design: Stephen H. Provost

The contents of this volume and all other works by Stephen H. Provost and Sharon Marie Provost are entirely the work of the authors, with the exception of direct quotations, attributed material used with permission, and items in the public domain. No artificial intelligence ("AI") programs were used to generate content in the creation of this work. No portion of this book, or any of the author's works, may be used to train or provide content for artificial intelligence (AI) programs.

All stories ©2024 Sharon Marie Provost
Dragon Crown Books 2024
All rights reserved.

ISBN: 978-1-949971-47-7

# Dedication

Dedicated to all the quiet, normal people out there who like to explore the dark and twisty side of life every now and then, even if it is only in the pages of a book.

*"We all go a little mad sometimes."*

— Norman Bates
*Psycho*, 1960

# Contents

| | |
|---|---|
| Foreword | 1 |
| Introduction & Acknowledgments | 3 |
| | |
| Solinsky Alley | 7 |
| Pease Porridge | 23 |
| More Than Skin Deep | 35 |
| Poseidon's Revenge | 51 |
| Phrogger | 63 |
| Hell's Bell | 109 |
| Lost in Time | 123 |
| Soulmates | 137 |
| Thanksgiving | 163 |
| Savage Nature | 175 |
| The Grandfather Paradox | 191 |

# Shadow's Gate

# Foreword

What does it take to be a good horror writer? First, and most obviously, you've got to be able to scare people. And one of the best ways to do that is to surprise them. Sharon Marie Provost has plenty of surprises in store for you in this, her debut solo collection of short stories.

You may be familiar with Sharon's work from her previous contributions to *The ACES Anthology* ("The Shining Night") and co-authorship with yours truly of another collection of dark tales, *Christmas Nightmare's Eve*. If you've read any of her previous material, you know you're in for a treat.

Too often, writers in this particular genre pin themselves down by offering a pastiche of clichés that are both derivative and predictable. You've read plenty of stories that feature gratuitous gore; the birth of the Antichrist; demonically possessed sisters in an isolated convent; and brain-dead zombies that amble about so slowly even Frankenstein's monster could outrun them... been there, read that.

But here's the thing about Sharon's work: She *has* written about zombies, and some of her stories are plenty bloody, but she knows how to step outside the same-old, same-old cardboard box of horror subgenres that you've read a thousand-and-one times before. One reason she can do this is she doesn't limit herself. She takes her inspiration from a wealth of sources: obscure medieval fables written to scare children into obedience; visits to frozen-in-time ghost towns; her own background studying police investigations and forensics... and much more. She's never running out of ideas.

Some of those ideas are brought to fruition on the pages

ahead. I'm flattered that may own collection of dark short stories and poems, *Nightmare's Eve*, was also one of her inspirations. But I can't take credit for launching her on this path: She's been a fan of horror books and movies all her life. So if you're wondering how a fortysomething former veterinary office manager has stepped so seamlessly into a new career as a horror author, it's really no mystery. She knows her stuff.

She's immersed herself in it and continues to do so, from stories by Stephen King and Richard Matheson to the *Scream* movies to *Black Mirror* and *The Twilight Zone*. And that's less than the tip of the iceberg. When you add to that her natural affinity for written communication—she's a fantastic technical writer—and her innate talent for storytelling, you've got a writer who can whip up everything from a spooky ghost story to a tension-filled slasher tale, from dark neo-mythology to a twist-filled paranormal love story.

She's also multitalented: The photographs on the cover of this book are hers, taken at one of the sites that inspired a story contained herein: Chinese Camp, California, the location of Solinsky Alley.

As her editor and collaborator, I'm thrilled to present this collection of short stories titled *Shadow's Gate*. I'm sure you'll enjoy stepping through that magical portal and into the shadowy realm of Sharon's imagination. Walk with her, if you dare, and explore the sometimes twisted, sometimes tragic, but always compelling tales drawn from the mind of Sharon Marie Provost. I'm proud to introduce to you the emerging queen of the horror short story.

*Stephen H. Provost*

*March 14, 2024*

# Introduction & Acknowledgments

Little did I know how much my life would change over the past three years. For twenty years, I enjoyed a rewarding career as an office manager at a veterinary hospital. Life was good, as I spent much of my free time reading, competing in dog sports with my poodles, and performing paranormal investigations. Vacations were spent visiting historical locations, such as Williamsburg and Petersburg, Virginia, as well as the wealth of local sites found here in Nevada.

Then, one day, my life changed drastically when I was diagnosed with Stage 4 cancer. The next few months were very difficult, as I underwent major surgery and started chemotherapy. I cannot possibly extend enough thanks to my mother, Roxanne Stora, who helped me during this difficult time.

Sick or not, I don't let anything get me down for too long, so I resumed my normal life activities very soon after my surgery. Oddly enough, six months later on a visit to a historical location to do some paranormal investigating, I met the man who would become my husband, Stephen H. Provost. He had written a favorite book of mine, a collection of short horror stories called *Nightmare's Eve*. I recognized him and introduced myself, and the rest, as they say, is history.

He moved here approximately six months later, and we were married just about a year after that. During this time, my

# Sharon Marie Provost

husband, Stephen, and my mother have been instrumental in keeping up my spirits and helping me with anything and everything I might need as I go through the difficult treatments. My husband and I have enjoyed many research trips, traveling across the entire state of Nevada, much of California and even parts of Oregon, as we gather information and photographs for his travel/highway history series of books.

My husband could see I needed an outlet, and in our conversations, he clearly noticed I had a creative side. He asked me to write a short story for his 2023 *ACES Anthology*, a collection of short stories from Northern Nevada writers. I approached this project with a degree of anxiety about whether I could write something that would be interesting to other people. However, as I pondered an idea for a story, I found myself thinking about the countless multitudes of horror books I had read, horror movies I had seen, and my interest in legends and mythologies around the world. And suddenly, an idea was born—as far as I can tell, a novel one at that.

From there, he persuaded me to co-author a book of Christmas-themed short horror stories with him, which we called *Christmas Nightmare's Eve*. Once the creative juices started flowing, and I became more confident and accustomed to writing, I found myself hooked. I have a list of story ideas just waiting to be written.

I have always been full of creative ideas, and as a child of 6, I wrote short horror stories—mostly about vampires. Did I mention my literal lifelong love of horror? But my love of animals came to exceed that of writing, so my life went down another path. Little did I know that one day I would have a husband who saw my potential and would persuade me to give it another try. I cannot possibly thank him enough for pushing

## Shadow's Gate

me to start writing again when I felt unsure. It has given me just the outlet I needed to pour out my frustrations and fears, while also exploring the dark and twisty (only on paper) side of me.

Once again, I must also acknowledge my mother who has supported me through every endeavor in my life and *always* told me I could do whatever I put my mind to.

Now I have a new career as a horror author that I absolutely adore. This book is a continuation of that *Nightmare's Eve* series that my husband created and which led to our meeting. What an honor to be entrusted with that mantle, as he focuses primarily on his nonfiction history books. I hope you will enjoy this journey with me as we travel to the other side... frequently dark but always supernatural.

*Sharon Marie Provost*

*March 16, 2024*

Sharon Marie Provost

Shadow's Gate

# Solinsky Alley

**B**elle navigated the curves and rolling hills on California State 49 in her Jeep Renegade as smoothly as if she were driving a Corvette. She was lost in thought at the prospect of exploring this ghost town that had been haunting her since the first moment she heard about it.

# Sharon Marie Provost

Something always seemed to get in the way, but finally she was *going* to see it.

Chinese Camp had been a booming commercial town situated near a junction of trails that led to a variety of mining towns in the area. It even became a major stop for stages and freight wagons on the way to those towns. A large population of Chinese miners had founded the town after being forced out of another camp in 1849. If that wasn't interesting enough, Chinese Camp had been the site of the first Tong war in the state of California, involving more than 2,500 people—four of whom lost their lives.

Belle almost missed her turn, and her tires kicked up the gravel at the edge of the highway as she made the rapid, sharp left turn onto Washington Street. She parked on the grassy edge of the road just past the entrance to the town. She knew she would find the majority of the historical buildings on Main Street, and she didn't want her modern car to ruin the aesthetics of her photos.

She started down Washington Street to investigate the old, abandoned homes there before moving on to the real heart of her obsession. She liked to immerse herself slowly and try to imagine herself in the once-bustling town. As she rounded the corner onto Red Hill Road, she could already see the wooden building that had once been the A. Gross Saloon. She swore she heard a cacophony of voices, in a variety of languages, talking and laughing about the exploits of the day as their beer mugs thumped onto the table.

Her steps slowed as she proceeded up Main Street, gaping at the large, old dance hall and house of ill-repute known as the Fandango House. She could hear the lively music pumping through the walls and the thumping of feet from girls dancing

# Shadow's Gate

the can-can. Next to the saloon, the west wall of the New York Store had collapsed. She made a mental note to climb over the wall and explore the ruins later. Then she looked across to the Robert Orford Store, surrounded by many of the Trees of Heaven brought over by the Chinese. The whole area was overgrown with the invasive species, which reproduced quickly and poisoned the soil, preventing the growth of other plants and trees.

Her eyes followed the shadow of a person walking from one store to the other making purchases for supper.

Just down the road from the crumbling store, she walked by the two-story Fox Boarding House, surrounded by towering, gnarled Trees of Heaven. She heard a woman hustling through, cleaning the rooms and preparing dinner for the hungry miners who would return to camp in the evening. In fact, one miner was headed this way after cutting down Solinsky Alley, the dirt path shortcut between Washington and Main Street.

Belle could almost see the Masonic Lodge that had once stood there next to the path. The only proof of its existence: a crumbling wall that stood next to a corrugated sheet metal garage. She smiled as she approached the last two buildings at the end of the street, the most impressive ones in town. A short distance from the Boarding House was the Morris Store with its two large and sturdy green iron doors.

Finally, Belle turned to stare, mouth agape, at the beautiful masonry work on the International Order of the Odd Fellows building on the corner. The awe-inspiring structure looked like it belonged on a vineyard in Italy. It was a pity that the front and much of the back of the building were hidden behind trees, underbrush and clinging ivy. Only the side of the building let her see the intricate detail work involved in its construction. Her eyes passed over the doors and windows, many hidden behind vines. They stopped dead when she saw the clear outline of a man's figure standing at an upstairs window, watching her.

Belle had always had an active imagination. This was not the first time that she had *experienced* a ghost town as she walked through it. Today's sensations were certainly more vivid than most, but this figure looked like an actual live person standing there. She jumped as a car flew by on the highway, only five feet from where she stood. When her eyes flicked back up, the figure had disappeared. She looked down at her watch as her stomach rumbled.

*How can it be 1 p.m. already? My initial walkthrough took an hour and a half! I'd better go eat before I start my documentation.*

Belle continued past the front of the I.O.O.F. building, alongside CA-49, and turned back down to her car. She opened the back and sat on the cargo bed to eat her lunch of a tuna sandwich, Sumo oranges and a granola bar. She grew warm in the sunlight shining down on her. When she finished eating, she grabbed her Yeti water bottle and her Canon camera bag containing a variety of lenses and filters. Then she locked the car back up to protect her video and other equipment. A group of rough-looking motorcyclists had passed by while she ate, and from the sounds of it were hanging out at the tavern in the Chinese Camp Store a quarter of a mile down the road.

She decided to take the shortcut through Solinsky Alley on her return to Main Street. Stopping a few feet down the path, she spent a few minutes photographing the yard and windmill behind the I.O.O.F building as well as a shed behind the Fandango House. As she stood there, a cool breeze picked up, and dark, gray storm clouds rolled in overhead. It gave the whole area an ominous, closed-in feeling. A chill ran down her spine, and she couldn't shake the feeling that she should turn

# Shadow's Gate

back.

*Get moving, you ninny! You will warm up once you start walking around and climbing through those ruins.*

As she neared the end of the path, she tripped and fell to her knees at the sound of a woman's scream to her right. She rose to her feet and turned to run at the sight of rapid movement in the brush coming right at her. A mad laugh erupted from her throat as she realized the scream and movement had come from a small group of peacocks she had startled during their courtship display. She had forgotten that Chinese Camp in the 21$^{st}$ century was primarily populated by wild peacocks rather than miners. She pulled a handkerchief out of her pocket and stanched the flow of blood from a cut on her knee before finishing her walk across the alley.

As her feet touched the road, the air stilled completely, and any sounds of the highway outside of town seemed to fade and even disappear. However, the feeling of being watched... no, stalked... returned.

*You are being ridiculous! There is nobody else out here in the old part of town. The only people nearby are the bikers drinking at the tavern.*

Belle shook her head and walked down toward Red Hill Road. She wanted to start with a wide-angle lens to document the entire street; then she walked down Main Street and stood with her back toward the highway to get it from the other direction. As she was taking the photos, she felt like someone running brushed against her from behind. She turned her head to see a shadow disappearing behind the Morris Store. The side door on the I.O.O.F. building was still slightly ajar.

*Fuck! There is someone out here messing with me! Now is it just a local kid or one of those bikers?*

Belle was determined that no one and nothing would

distract her from her work. She refused to succumb to their scare tactics, so she continued to take pictures as if she hadn't been bothered. She took advantage of the open door on the I.O.O.F. building to enter and document whatever items might have been left behind. She was descending the stairs after checking out the second floor when she heard someone enter the building from a back door.

She hastened her step and left through the side door, closing it behind her.

She walked through the jungle that was the front yard taking what pictures she could get of the front of the building. A car horn honked, and the driver waved as he drove past on the highway. Belle smiled and waved back as she moved around the far side of the building and out into the back yard, photographing the old windmill as she went by. As she crossed the field in back to return to Main Street, she heard someone moving through the brush paralleling her path. She casually turned toward the sound as she took pictures looking down Solinsky Alley toward Washington Street, and she saw someone dart back inside the building.

Belle circled the Morris Store, photographing it from every angle before heading down to the Fox Boarding House. She entered through the unlocked front door and wedged a board under the door handle to prevent someone from entering behind her. She spent the next hour wandering the house and documenting everything she found.

As she rounded the corner of the boarding house, she saw movement approaching her rapidly from the back side of the building. She turned toward it and met the man with a resounding *thwack* from a blow with the heavy Maglite flashlight she carried in her pack. Then she took off running

# Shadow's Gate

past the man writhing on the ground, into the trees and underbrush behind the buildings. She ran past the New York Store, then quietly climbed into the ruins through the crumbled west wall. Belle crawled through the debris, cutting her hands and knees on bits of tin and broken glass, until she was out of sight. She fought to slow her breathing, so she wouldn't give herself away.

He was so stealthy that she never heard or saw him approach.

He yanked Belle's head up by her ponytail, slamming it off a piece of sheet metal that cut her forehead. He turned and began to drag her through the scrap, but lost his grip on her hair as he tried to pull her up and over the wall. That was all the break she needed. Belle jumped away and ran toward the Chinese Camp Store at the opposite end of town, bellowing for help. Branches whipped against her skin, raising welts.

Belle heard the voices of the raucous bikers who had moved out to the fenced garden on the side of the store. She let out a bloodcurdling scream, as if her life depended on it; she was beginning to think it just might. Just as she reached the fence, she pitched forward hard when the assailant tackled her from behind, knocking the wind out of her.

A weak "oomph" issued from her lips.

She struggled to take another breath, but her diaphragm refused to respond. Her head began to swim from oxygen deprivation. Utter blackness descended over her vision, but Belle refused to give in.

"Did you hear that?" the burly red-haired biker asked from his seat on the bench.

His girl sat next to him, wearing a *Biker Babe* T-shirt,

alongside her friend. "What, babe?" she said.

"That scream. A woman screamed... right beside us... on the other side of this fence."

"Biker Babe" and her friend tittered, slapping their thighs in delight, as much at his ignorance as their amusement.

"Don't you know anything? Didn't you see them as we entered town? Chinese Camp is full of wild peacocks. It's mating season. The males shake their tail feathers and call out to their gals. It sounds like a woman screaming."

"Biker Babe's" friend stood up to stretch. The large biker with the greasy beard slapped her on the ass hard as he guffawed, "It is the woman's job to shake her tail feathers for me. Do that right, and I will make you scream."

"Ooohh yes, baby!" she exclaimed as she shook her round ass in his face.

Belle's eyes began to blink as the hazy image of her surroundings came into view. She realized with a start that she must have passed out, because she was lying on the floor in one of the back rooms of the I.O.O.F. building.

"Hello there, sleepyhead."

Belle sat up and turned to look behind her. She scrambled backward against the wall as she saw a tall man with dark brown hair and green piercing eyes staring at her, his expression tinged with malice. He sat at the table, a large Bowie knife in his hand. The tip was buried in the tabletop as he slowly spun it in place.

"Why do you have that? Please don't hurt me," she whimpered, her gaze unflinching as she stayed focused on his movements.

"This little thing?" He held up the knife, brandishing it at

# Shadow's Gate

her.

"Please let me go. I won't tell anybody about you. I'll just leave, and you'll never see or hear from me again."

"I can do that. I *will* make sure that you are never seen or heard from again."

"Those bikers are probably looking for me now. They must have heard my scream."

"Nobody is looking for you. They don't even know you were there... not really. Besides, they couldn't find you if they tried."

"What do you mean?"

"You are no longer on the same plane of existence as they are."

Belle looked at him, unsure of what to think.

The man continued: "Two different planes overlap here," he said, his tone betraying both impatience and boredom. " The wall on this side is very thin. You can see and hear everything on both sides, but you can't cross back over. The other side can't see you. They might hear whispers of you, but they would not be clear."

"What are you talking about? That doesn't make any sense. Are you out of your mind? I am trapped... here... right now, but I could leave if I got to my car. The only reason the bikers wouldn't be able to understand me is that they're too drunk.

"Why are you holding me here? What are you going to do to me?"

"I am not the one holding you here. *It* is the one holding you."

"What the actual fuck? It? What is *it*? Who is *it*?"

"Chinese Camp."

"I know where we are. What is your point?"

"Chinese Camp is holding you here... not me. I am in the same boat as you. It is holding me here as well. I have just learned how to take lemons and make lemonade."

"You are fucking insane! The fucking town is holding me here? Yeah! Sure! That is reasonable."

"You know the history of the place, don't you? You seemed to know what you were doing when you were walking around, investigating the town."

"Yes, I do."

"Chinese Camp was a busy town at the center of several mining booms. Thousands of people lived here. Then one day the mines dried up, and they all left. The town fell into ruin as time and weather took their toll on all these places at the center of life here. Ever wonder why they're called ghost towns? The towns themselves have a spirit... an essence. That spirit became despondent and, dare I say, lonely."

"That is ridiculous!"

"People visit here every single day. As they drive by on the highway, they see the town and stop to investigate. But then they leave, just like all the others. The town tried to create a feeling... an experience... for those who visited to keep them interested. It worked to a degree; paranormal investigators were drawn here to investigate the strange phenomena people encountered, but they, too, left after a day or so. So it came up with a different solution... a quite innovative one, if you ask me."

"And what is that?"

"It created a portal that, once crossed, does not let you cross back over. It traps you here, building up its population once again with townspeople who cannot abandon it."

"What portal? I went back to my car earlier, and I could have left then."

# Shadow's Gate

"True. You could have... you should have, but you did not. You hadn't crossed the portal yet, but you did when you returned after lunch. I saw it on your face when you felt it. I was watching and waiting—hoping—you would make that fateful mistake. You see, I couldn't do anything to you until you were on this side. You could hear and see me, but just faintly—never enough to make you afraid... that is, until you joined me on the flip side."

"Are you talking about when I walked down Solinsky Alley? When the wind came up as the storm clouds rolled in? There was nothing supernatural about it."

"Yes, there was, and you know it. The portal is crossed when you travel through Solinsky Alley from Washington to Main Street. I know you felt that same feeling of being closed in. I know you had that sense of foreboding, warning you to turn back. I saw how nervous you were when you got to the other side because you could feel me. You knew I was here in that moment."

"And the wind stopped instantly..."

"Exactly! That was the moment you became a permanent resident of Chinese Camp."

"Oh my God! What did you mean about making lemonade out of lemons when it comes to you living here?"

"I should start by explaining a few things. I have an overwhelming compulsion to kill young women. I love to bathe myself in their blood when I slit their throats. Chopping them into little bits gives me pleasure," he growled as he ran his hand down his body suggestively.

Belle began to sob with great wracking gasps for air. Rivulets of snot ran down her face, and she used the back of her hand to wipe them away. As he stood and approached her, she collapsed into a heap on the floor, pulling her legs up into the fetal position. Her overwhelmed mind couldn't even devise a plan to fight off her assailant.

"No! Don't you dare do that! You can't shut down on me now. Do you hear me? You must hear me out, or I will cause you pain like you can't possibly imagine. Just when you think your mind and body will give out from the never-ending waves of pain, I will increase it until pain is your whole world. Your mind may break, but you will still feel pain until I *decide* it is time for *me* to break your body. And it will not be quick. I will keep you alive for weeks. You are mine now! Do you get it? Are you ready to listen again?"

"Uh huh," she mumbled as her eyes remained glazed over.

"I saw a young woman here alone, much like you were. No one else was around. Even the Chinese Camp Store was closed that day. She was parked on Main Street and so engrossed in taking selfies she never even noticed me drive by, staring at her. I parked on Washington and cut through Solinsky Alley, coming up behind her. I slashed her tires and began my game of stalking her. She even made it down to the store and ran out into the highway, nearly getting herself hit by a car. Fortunately, they thought she was drunk and did not stop to help her. When I was done having fun, I caught her and tortured her until she begged me to kill her. I did... a few weeks and a couple of pints of blood later."

"So you kill the people who get stuck here? That is your definition of lemonade? If Chinese Camp is trying to rebuild its population, then don't you anger it when you kill the people it has trapped? What happens to them? Are they freed from this plane?"

"Oh God no! Their spirits are still stuck here, but I get to have my fun at least. Once you cross the portal, your spirit

# Shadow's Gate

remains here whether you are alive or dead. You and I are still alive... at least for now you are... but neither of us will ever leave here. You will meet the spirits, well, more like *see* them, eventually. They like to hide."

Belle had been lost in her mind, spiraling through pain, fear, and angst. She kept picturing her mother, who would be lost without her. She knew she couldn't give up, for her sake. Her anger built until it surpassed all those other feelings. She sat up, glaring up at him, her brow furrowed. "You're insane! I will not let you do this to me. I am leaving here *now*," she spat at him as she rose.

He laughed with glee; his eyes dancing with merriment. "Okay, rabbit. Run, little rabbit, run! If you are so sure you can get away, go do it. I will even give you a head start."

As a former sprinter in high school, Belle was off like a shot had rung out from the starter's pistol. She burst out the front door, slamming it behind her. She took off toward the highway, bursting out onto the pavement as her eyes searched wildly for any car that might come along. But as her feet hit the pavement, she found herself standing on the rough potholed road that was Main Street in front of the Gross Saloon. There he was, leaning against the back doorjamb—the amusement apparent in his eyes.

She ran toward the Chinese Camp Store again, except this time she ran around the fence and into the garden. "Help me!" she screamed as she came to a halt in front of "Biker Babe" and her man. Neither one looked at her. They just kept laughing as she sat on his lap and began to rub his chest. Belle reached out to slap her face, but she never made contact. Her hand just appeared on the other side.

Belle jumped when she heard his voice right behind her.

# Sharon Marie Provost

"You convinced yet?"

"Never!"

Belle ran past him and headed west toward some of the newer homes that were still inhabited, but she never made it. As her feet reached the far edge of Red Hill Road, she was transported back to the Orford Store. Her back arched as she felt the tip of his knife against her lower back.

"Don't move! I am done playing this cat and mouse game. I may still be alive, but I am not bound by the normal rules of physics here. I can appear at will anywhere I like... at least within the confines of Chinese Camp. There is no escape."

"I agree. I am done with your sick little game," she groaned defiantly as she leaned back, slipping the knife between her ribs and burying it in her kidney. She twisted her body around to face him, creating a large gash across her body.

"Game over," she wheezed as she collapsed into his arms, blood pouring onto the ground and soaking into the barren soil.

The young woman pulled into the Chinese Camp Store lot. She had a lot on her mind as she contemplated whether she was going to marry Chad or go to grad school before settling on her future. She walked in to get an energy drink as she contemplated her next step. She was going to sit in the garden, but the sounds of the power saw being used to rebuild the fence were grating on her nerves. She decided to walk along the highway and go into the historical district to explore while she called her parents to set their mind at ease.

As she walked down the street, she kept seeing a shadow dart amongst the trees, following her every move. The movements became more frantic as she approached a dirt path through the middle of the south side of Main Street. She

# Shadow's Gate

continued down the road and then turned around as she hung up her phone.

When she approached the path, she saw a large puddle of blood on the ground as she heard a faint spine-chilling scream of agony. The shadow darted past her again, nearly knocking her over as she jumped aside.

"Run! Get out of here *now!* He will kill you," Belle screamed next to the young woman's ear, hoping she would at least get a feeling of dread and danger. He ran at her, trying to push her away, but she was too fast for him. "So help me, you will never have another victim. Chinese Camp is just going to have to deal with the current population. There is no room for any more."

The young woman couldn't explain her experiences, but she didn't care. She wasn't going to stick around long enough to find out. She jogged up the street and then down the highway back to her car. Her car sped past the abandoned, yet not uninhabited, I.O.O.F. building as she headed back home to make her decision in safety.

The Chinese Camp Store continued to do a booming business, providing drinks and snacks for the weary traveler, but the historic section of town had few visitors that never seemed to stay for very long.

# Sharon Marie Provost

# Shadow's Gate

# Pease Porridge

"Mary, I need to go out. Mrs. Appleton's baby is coming, and she sent her daughter to get me. I started the fire to reheat the leftover stew in the kettle from last night. Can you get some milk from the goat, then add it to the stew along with some oats to make breakfast for your father and our guest? And help feed your little sister when she wakes."

"Do we have any bacon, Mother?"

"No, darling. Hopefully, I will get paid for my midwife duties today, and I will try to stop by the market to pick up some meat."

"Yes, mother. I will see you later."

Mrs. Abbott grabbed her satchel of supplies, rushed out of the house, and ran across the village. The daughter had appeared quite worried when she came to ask for help. She said Mrs. Appleton was in great pain, and there was some bleeding.

*I hope this birth goes well. I need this money to feed my family. Times have been hard, and food has been short. With Mr. Edwards visiting, I have another mouth to feed with the same scant amount of food.*

As she rounded the corner of the hovel, she heard a scream from inside. Elspeth was waiting for her at the door, wringing her hands.

"Please hurry, Mrs. Abbott."

Mrs. Abbott rushed to the cot in the back corner. There was quite a lot of blood staining the bedsheet. Mrs. Appleton appeared pale and weak. Mrs. Abbott began to palpate her abdomen, worry apparent on her face.

"Don't fret now, Mrs. Appleton. We will get this taken care of, but we have an issue. The baby is facing the wrong direction. I need to help turn the baby, but this is going to hurt... a lot. Elspeth, give me that wood spoon for Mrs. Appleton to bite down on."

Elspeth placed the spoon between Mrs. Appleton's teeth, and then sat down beside her, placing her hands on her mother's shoulders to hold her down. Mrs. Abbott placed one hand on top of her abdomen and used the other to reach in and slowly turn the baby. As she started to do so, she felt the umbilical cord pull taut. She turned the baby back in the other direction a bit and slid the cord from around the baby's neck. Then she began the tedious task of turning the baby's body head-down once again. After what felt like hours, the baby was finally in place for Mrs. Appleton to begin pushing.

"I know you are tired, Mrs. Appleton, but I need you to push hard with the next contraction."

Two long, painful pushes later, the baby boy was delivered,

# Shadow's Gate

blue and motionless. Mrs. Abbott wrapped him in a towel and turned to the table. She laid him down upon it, rubbing his little body vigorously as she cleared his little mouth. She patted him on the back and gave him a few small breaths. Noticing how quiet the room had become, she looked over at Mrs. Appleton, trying to erase her frown, as she asked, "How are you doing, Mrs. Appleton?"

"I think she is unconscious, Mrs. Abbott," Elspeth said.

"Is she breathing?"

"Yes, ma'am. She is still bleeding though."

Mrs. Abbott, realizing that there was no hope for the little boy, placed him on the table and turned back to the mother.

"I will do what I can to help your mother," she told Elspeth. "She is very sick right now. She has lost a lot of blood. You need to see if you can find the healer."

Mrs. Abbot began massaging the abdomen, trying to help the uterus expel the afterbirth and then stanch the flow of blood. After some time, the blood slowed to a trickle and stopped. Elspeth returned and reported that the healer would be arriving in minutes. Mrs. Abbott had Elspeth help her change the sheet underneath Mrs. Appleton and then covered her with a warm blanket. She swaddled the baby in another blanket and covered its face before turning to Elspeth.

"Your mother is very weak right now. We need to minimize her stress. This will be hard enough for her as it is. I will take care of burying the baby. Keep your mother warm and still until the healer arrives. Is your father at the market?"

"Yes, ma'am, he is. I didn't even have a chance to tell him that the baby was coming."

"I will go talk to him. Tell your mother I am so sorry. Let her know that it was not her fault. Tell her God called his angel home early."

# Sharon Marie Provost

Their village was so small, it had neither a church nor an official cemetery. Mrs. Abbott grabbed a small spade outside the home and walked into the forest to the spot where the villagers laid their loved ones to rest. She stopped at the nearby creek to prepare the body and interred him a short while later. She stopped by the hovel to return the spade, just as the healer was leaving.

"Thank you, Mrs. Abbott. You did a remarkable job of caring for her... the best you could, given the circumstances."

"Is she going to recover?"

"It is touch and go at this point, but I do believe so. She is a strong woman. It is all up to God now. I will be back to check on her later."

Mrs. Abbott proceeded to the market, sorrowful but hopeful that she would be able to take care of her family that night. She found Mr. Appleton at his farmstand in the market. He looked up, surprised to see her.

"Mr. Abbott, I need to speak to you. Your daughter came to get me earlier because the baby was coming. There were complications, and your son was stillborn. Your wife is very weak from blood loss. The healer has been by already and will be coming back later."

"And my son? We were going to name him Lee."

"I buried him in the village plot. I didn't know what you were going to call him, so I didn't mark the grave. It is under the willow tree in the back corner. I just didn't want to upset your wife by seeing him when she awoke."

"I understand. Thank you, Mrs. Abbott. You are a godsend."

Mrs. Abbott returned home, a small bundle in her hands.

"Momma, did you get bacon?" little Elsa asked, licking her lips.

# Shadow's Gate

"No, dear. I couldn't afford it. But I did the best I could and brought home a small bit of roast."

Mary frowned as she asked, "Did the Appletons not pay you? You were gone for hours, Momma."

"Times are tough for everyone, Mary. And today, their lot is even more heartbreaking. Mrs. Appleton's son was stillborn. She is very ill, and they will have to pay the healer as well. I did the best I could and brought this home for our dinner tonight."

"I see, Momma. I will hang it over the hearth to roast."

"Mary, can you take your sister out to play while you pick some peas and dig up some potatoes and carrots for the stew tonight?"

"Yes, mother."

Mrs. Abbott spent the next couple of hours tidying the home and then cleaning and preparing the vegetables for the stew that night. The roast, although small, smelled delicious and was cooking up nicely on the spit by the hearth. Mrs. Abbott turned as their guest, Mr. Edwards, entered the room.

"Hello, Mrs. Abbott. It smells marvelous in here! How are you today? I heard you had to run out of here early this morning to deliver a baby."

"Yes, I did. The wee little babe was stillborn. Mrs. Appleton is quite weak, but I hope she will recover soon. I buried him in the village burial plot. I just couldn't let her wake up and see him."

"How dreadful! They were very lucky to have you help them so. I will be back in a few hours for that delicious dinner you are preparing, I must attend to some work with your husband and with some other villagers in town before my departure later this week. I guess I will have to delay my meeting with Mr. Appleton for a couple of days."

"See you later, Mr. Edwards."

## Sharon Marie Provost

"Oh, Mrs. Abbott, did the little lad have a name? I thought it might be a nice gesture if I had a little marker made for his grave. I can give it to Mr. Appleton when I meet with him."

"His name was Lee."

"Thank you."

Mrs. Abbott checked on her garden and played with Elsa. She sent Mary into the village to check on Mrs. Appleton and was pleased to hear she seemed to be improving. Before long, her husband arrived home, followed closely by Mr. Edwards. The men washed up for dinner as Mary and Mrs. Abbott set the table. The family sat down to dinner and delighted in the best dinner they'd had in weeks. With their garden being so small, they rarely had the variety and quantity of vegetables in their stew that they did that night, but Mrs. Abbott was determined to impress their guest. They devoured the small roast. Circumstances today had allowed them to enjoy this rare delicacy in their happy but poor household.

Elsa ate like a bird as usual and asked to be excused to play with her dolls by the hearth. The adults sipped mead while engaged in lively conversation, as Mary cleaned up the dinner dishes. Mr. Edwards turned his head towards Elsa, a wistful smile on his face, as he listened to her sing nursery rhymes.

> "Lee's porridge hot, Lee's porridge cold,
> Lee's porridge in the pot, nine days old;
> Some like it hot, some like it cold,
> Some like it in the pot, nine days old."

Mr. Edwards chuckled and said, "Dear Elsa, silly little girl. It is *pease* porridge hot, *pease* porridge cold. It is about a stew, or porridge, made with peas and vegetables, much like we had

# Shadow's Gate

tonight."

"No... no... no... nooooooo! It was Lee's porridge. He was yummy."

"What? Whatever do you mean by that? Lee... Lee... why does that sound so familiar?"

Mrs. Abbott jumped up, her hands shaking, as she stammered, "Elsa! You... you... don't kn... know what you are talking about. You are confused."

Mr. Edwards' eyes flicked back and forth between Mrs. Abbott and her husband, questioning.

Mr. Abbott scoffed and said, "She is young and impressionable. She must have heard Nora and Mary talking about the loss of the Appleton's poor little babe, Lee. The money she earned allowed us to purchase that delicious roast Nora made. Am I right, Nora?"

"Of course, of course. They were both here when I arrived home, and Mary asked if I had been able to buy bacon. I thought she was playing, but she must have overhead us talking. She gets confused by adult conversations all the time."

Mary left the dishes and shooed Elsa to the back of the cottage and behind the curtain where their beds were located. She put her to bed, told her a story and then returned to finish the dishes for her mother. The adults' conversation had restarted, but the air was still awkward. When they all retired for the night, Mrs. Abbott apologized again for Elsa's impertinent behavior.

"I really wanted you to have a good impression of us. I love my little girl, but I hate to admit she is a little slow."

"Think nothing of it, Mrs. Abbott. I was not offended. Goodnight then."

The next day, Mr. Edwards rose to find the whole family just sitting down to breakfast, except for Elsa. He could hear her playing behind the curtain in the back. The family's behavior was still tense, and they seemed very concerned about maintaining normal appearances. Mr. Edwards ate a small bite and then excused himself to begin his work with some of the other villagers.

Mr. Edwards finished his business dealings with the other villagers early. He stopped by the carpenter's shop to check on the small wooden cross he had commissioned to mark Lee Appleton's grave and was told it would be ready later that afternoon. As he exited the shop, he saw Mr. Appleton at his stand and decided to stop by to set up a meeting time with him.

"Hello, Mr. Appleton. My deepest condolences to you and your family. I am staying with the Abbotts and heard about the passing of your dear son."

"Thank you, Mr. Edwards. That is very kind of you. I suppose you are here to discuss business."

"Not now... I want to give you some time. I am here for a few more days, so I thought I would drop by to set up a time that was convenient for you."

"That is very considerate. Would Friday morning work for you? My son will be here working the stand, so I can meet you at the pub at 9."

"Yes, that would be perfect. By the way, I commissioned a small grave marker for Lee. I will bring it to you on Friday, so your family can place it and have a small service when your wife recuperates. Also, I would like to reimburse you for what you paid Mrs. Abbott for her services. I know this is a challenging time for your family, and funds must be short, with having to pay the healer as well."

"I didn't pay Mrs. Abbott yet. I explained to her that business has been slow lately. Our gardens have not produced much between the rabbits and the insect infestation. I told her I would pay her as soon as our circumstances improved."

Mr. Edwards' brow furrowed as he replied, "Oh... oh, I am sorry. I must have misunderstood. Well, I will speak to her then and take care of it as I said."

"You are much too kind, sir. My family will be forever indebted to you. G'day, sir."

Mr. Edwards couldn't get the conversation out of his mind, nor could he forget the eerie words of Elsa.

*She was so emphatic. The Abbotts said the roast was purchased with money she earned from caring for Mrs. Appleton. But dear God, the alternative is monstrous. It just can't be.*

Mr. Edwards knew he could not put the matter behind him until he solved the mystery, one way or the other. He asked one of the villagers for directions to where the villagers bury people in the woods. It was a short walk, and he found the small grave without difficulty. The soil was still loose, so he was able to unearth the body easily. The sight he beheld was unimaginable. There was a small body of a newborn, as expected. However, the butchery perpetrated upon the body was beyond comprehension. The muscles and flesh of the buttocks had formed the majority of that roast the family had ingested the night before. Chunks of flesh had been carved out of the baby's chubby cheeks and upper thighs as well. He could feel his pulse pounding in his temple as his head throbbed. He turned to the side and retched his meager breakfast and bile until his throat burned.

He re-covered the body and pressed the soil down. He could not let that poor family see what had been done to their child.

Mr. Edwards debated how to handle the situation. This

village was so small it had not chosen a sheriff. He would have to travel several hours' ride to the next village to summon one.

*Surely, Jonathan doesn't know what his wife has done. He is a respectable man. I will tell him and maybe we can convince Nora to turn herself in.*

Mr. Edwards returned to the Abbott home. When he entered, he found Mrs. Abbott preparing dinner. He gagged as his thoughts returned to what he had just seen. She turned to greet him and smiled.

"How was your day, Mr. Edwards? I will have dinner done shortly."

"It went well. I have completed most of my dealings here. I will be moving on to Frampton in the next few days. I… I talked to Mr. Appleton today."

Mrs. Abbott stiffened and paused in her activities, as she asked, "Oh, yes? How is the family doing?"

"Mrs. Appleton is getting better. She will be up and about soon. A funny thing happened though. I asked him how much he had paid you because I wanted to reimburse him. I know their financial situation is difficult right now. He said that he hadn't paid you anything yet."

"Yes, that is correct."

"But your husband said, and you agreed, that you had bought the roast with the money you earned from treating Mrs. Appleton."

"I know. I know. We are having significant financial hardship as well. We are struggling to feed our own children. I couldn't tell my husband that I had agreed that they could pay me later."

"Well, how did you get the meat then? You know what else I did today? I took a stroll out to little Lee's gravesite. I bet you can tell me what I saw."

Mr. Abbott wrapped an arm around Mr. Edwards from behind, holding a knife to his throat, as he growled, "That is quite enough, Mr. Edwards. Why couldn't you just leave this alone? Everything would have been fine if you had just minded your own business."

"You knew? I told myself that you couldn't possibly know of your wife's monstrous misdeeds. You are a righteous man. These deeds go against all that is right and holy."

"There is nothing righteous or holy about this God that everyone prays to. He would not let my family suffer and nearly starve as we have. You have seen the challenging times facing this whole village... plague, poverty, infestations. He wouldn't make a family suffer as he did by taking a newborn child, as he did with Lee. We took a tragedy and turned it into a miracle for my family."

"You are sick and twisted. This is an abomination."

At that moment, Elsa skipped across the room laughing, as she said, "I toooooooold you!"

Mrs. Abbott approached him with a smile. "Now my family will benefit from another miracle. We thank you for your sacrifice. You will feed my family for quite some time. We can salt and smoke the meat to make it last."

Elsa was playing with her dolls by the fire again. She giggled and then looked up with a gleam in her eye as she chanted, "Edwards porridge hot, Edwards porridge cold, Edwards porridge in the pot nine days old."

# Sharon Marie Provost

Shadow's Gate

# More Than Skin Deep

*I am so disgusting! Totally, undeniably ugly! Everyone says I am beautiful on the inside. Well, beauty is in the eye of the beholder, and all there is to behold is my repulsive face and my boyish form. No voluptuous curves or full bosom.*

Perched on the edge of the chair, Emily found herself in tears once again. Her 35th birthday would soon be here, and she still had not found a man to love her. Hell, she would settle for an actual date at this point. She'd never had a boyfriend or a date to prom. Her mother had arranged the only so-called date she'd ever been on. She'd bribed Billy Adams with a one-year membership to the family fun center her family owned in exchange for taking Emily out to a movie and ice cream afterwards.

Emily had grown tired of the pitying looks people gave her when she tried to dress cute in the latest style. One more question or comment when she went out like, "Oh, dinner alone tonight, Em?" or "Tickets are two for one tonight... uhh... never mind, Em," and she was seriously going to lose it. Visions ran through her mind of spinning around to scream, "Yes! Of course, I am alone. I am always alone! Hello, Claire? This is not the first time we have gone through this charade."

Instead, she always calmed answered, "Thanks for the thought, Claire, but I only need one," or "Yep, just me tonight." She was tired of being meek and mild. Tired of trying to make everyone else feel better about making her feel like pond scum... the lowest of the low... scum of the earth.

*People are so fucking condescending! Then... THEN they have the guts to feel superior because they pity me. They look down on me from their towering high horse and throw me a few niceties. Pretend they are my friend. All hail, the benevolent Claire or Sam, or better yet, my "best friend" Allison.*

*I know Allison talks about me behind my back. Our friendship is based on her empty-nest boredom and her need to still feel hot, desired and adored. When men see us together, of course she receives all the attention. When women see us together, they are impressed by her charity, spending time with someone so far below her station in life. It is win-win for her, no matter what.*

*I hate myself even more because I know all this, but I still spend time with her. It gets so lonely without friends or a lover. Even though, we spend most of our time together talking about Allison's life, I can pretend, in the*

# Shadow's Gate

*moment, that we are actually having an enjoyable conversation.*

Staring at herself in the vanity mirror, Emily knew it was time for a change, but she didn't know how to go about that. She had been on a diet for five years straight. She really wasn't fat—just a few extra pounds. The problem was the weight wasn't distributed to the right locations in the right proportions. The only curve her body made was up from her shoulders to her thin neck. She likened her body to that of an awkward teenaged boy. Her plain-Jane face needed some serious plastic surgery, as did her breasts.

*I am not a fixer-upper—more like a bulldoze and rebuild.*

If she wanted to find a husband and build a family, Emily knew she was running out of time. Drastic change was needed, and this morning she might have finally found it. As she was crying in the mirror, she had the television on low for company. The words being spoken sent a quiver of excitement down her spine:

"Are you tired of your sad and lonely existence?

Are you unable to spend one more day looking at your reflection in the mirror?

If only you could find a way to be beautiful and desirable like Pamela Anderson... your life would be complete. Beauty, wealth, a family, and friends—now you can have all that.

The brilliant scientists at Métamorphose have developed a groundbreaking new treatment.

Now anyone... even you... can have the life you have always dreamed of.

We have payment plans available.

Call us today to schedule your appointment."

*This can't be possible, It has to be another one of those stupid informercials.*

# Sharon Marie Provost

Emily sprinted across the room to her diary on the bedside table, desperate to jot down the phone number before the commercial ended. She felt elated and nervous at the same time; she was scared to hope that she could finally have everything she had always dreamed about. She didn't even realize she had picked up the phone and dialed the number until a voice on the other end of the line said, "Thank you for calling Métamorphose, where you, too, can transform into a butterfly. My name is Giselle. How may I help you?"

"Hi... uh, I mean hello. My name is Emily. I... I... I am really sorry. Maybe this is a mistake."

"Transformation is never a mistake, Emily. Are you ready to bloom? We can help you with that."

"Yes. I do want that. Is it really true? Is the change as dramatic as the commercial implied? This is not just simple plastic surgery, right? I don't want to have my face destroyed like Michael Jackson. I have heard horror stories about botched nose jobs with the cartilage showing through the skin. Never mind. I am sorry. That was really rude."

"No, *mon cher*. I understand. This is completely different, I assure you. This is much more than plastic surgery. The results will be nothing short of extraordinary. We have truly developed a groundbreaking method of transformation. We are so excited about this treatment and convinced that you will be satisfied, that we offer a free consultation. How does your schedule look next Wednesday, the 5th, at 3 p.m.?"

"Umm... wow. That is really quick. That would be fine with me. So, there is truly no cost?"

"*Oui, madame*. Do you have specific trouble spots that need fixed or are you looking for more of a full-body makeover? Is there a specific person you want to look like?"

# Shadow's Gate

"Well yes, I would like to look like my best friend Allison. She has a beautiful face with perfectly proportioned features. She has curves in all the right places, and her breasts are to die for, plump and pert."

"*Magnifique, mon cher*. That certainly makes it easier for us. Do you have pictures of her that you can bring to your consultation? Obviously, we would need a full body shot, along with a head shot and profile photo. We will take many high-resolution photos of you to determine your bone structure. Then, using the latest AI software, we can create images of how you would appear with her facial and body features on your personal body structure. I am sure you will be very pleased with the outcome."

"That all sounds very exciting and high-tech. I can definitely bring those pictures with me. I can't wait for my appointment. Thank you so much, Giselle."

Emily spent the next week poring through pictures of Allison. She needed to pick the perfect ones that displayed her body in the most flattering fashion. Next, she went through her finances with a fine-tooth comb. She was determined to cut corners in her budget wherever possible and pull her retirement if needed to qualify for the treatment. She had neglected to ask the cost of such a procedure—not that they would have answered anyhow. The cost probably varied widely depending on how extensive it was.

*With all my flaws, I will be lucky if I can afford to have half my body overhauled.*

She had been champing at the bit all week, desperate to tell someone about the appointment but afraid they would try to dissuade her. The night before her appointment, her willpower finally broke down when she was on the phone with Allison. They had spent the last hour discussing Allison's new promotion and her flirtation with a co-worker.

"Allison, I have to tell you some exciting news."

"I really need to get going, but I guess I can spare a moment. What's so big?"

Emily could hear the sarcasm dripping with every word in that little question, punctuated by a snarky giggle at the end.

"Have you seen that commercial for Métamorphose?"

"I think I have heard something with that name. Why?"

"I have an appointment there tomorrow. They have some groundbreaking technology to transform you into the beautiful woman you have always dreamed of. Finally, I will be able to feel good about myself. Find a husband. Build a life that I can be proud of."

Allison's derisive laugh echoed through the phone, cutting Emily to the bone. Emily could picture the sneer on her face as she said, "Transformation! Are you joking? Be careful, little butterfly, that they don't wrap you in a chrysalis and leave you hidden there... the modern-day fat woman housecoat."

"I... I... never mind. It was a stupid idea. I should let you go."

"Sorry, Em. That was a bit rude of me. I just hate to see you waste your money and pin your hopes on some pie-in-the-sky miracle. I love you and all, but we both know it would take just such a miracle to make you beautiful. Your beauty is on the inside."

"Mm hmm. You are right as usual, Allison. I can always count on you to set me straight."

Emily hung up the phone, feeling sorrier for herself than ever. She might not have beauty, but she certainly had brains. She prided herself on that.

# Shadow's Gate

*Maybe I am just deluding myself. But... then again, it couldn't hurt just to go to the consultation. It is free, after all.*

Emily telecommuted for her job, so she rose early to get her day's work in before her appointment. Responsibility was important to her, and besides, working helped her pass the time while she anxiously awaited her appointment. At 2 p.m., she clocked out, gathered her pictures and left for the long drive across the city.

They were located at the far end of the business district, where all the tech companies had set up shop. She pressed the intercom, announcing herself, so she could pass through the immense gothic gates. A high brick wall surrounded the large property, enclosing a lush forest that hid their office from view. As she drove up the long, winding drive, she was shocked to see the sleek, modern building peeking through the trees. The facade was composed entirely of dark-tinted glass windows. Emily saw a row of visitor parking spaces in front, and chose one near the entrance.

She sat in the car with her eyes closed for a moment, trying to still her racing heart. When she opened her eyes again, she found a woman holding the front door open with a large, beckoning smile on her face. Emily returned her smile and quickly got herself together to exit the car.

"*Bonjour*, Emily! Welcome to Métamorphose. We are so happy you could join us."

"Thank you very much. Giselle, I presume?"

"*Oui, oui*. It is very nice to meet you. Let me get you settled into our consultation suite. I will have you change into one of our special jumpsuits. They give you a little privacy, while letting our cameras accurately photograph your body structure.

Then one of our technicians will be right in to walk you through the body-mapping photography. Do you have those pictures so I can get them input into the system?"

"Yes. Here you go. Will I get to speak with a doctor to discuss the process and... uh the cost?"

"Of course, Madame Emily. After the photos of you are finished, you will be able to change back into your clothes and enjoy some refreshments while the doctor looks over the findings and the AI program generates your results. As soon as he is ready, in probably 15 minutes or so, he will be in to show you the "new you" and discuss all the details. How does that sound?"

"That sounds perfect. I am really quite excited."

A special jumpsuit was one way to describe it. Emily's worst nightmare might be more accurate. It was more like a giant pair of nylons that fit your entire body. It did not cover anything except her nipples and groin, and it fit like a glove. There was no hiding any imperfections, but it certainly did accurately depict her body structure that way. She tried to disappear into her own thoughts while listening for the technician's instructions. Time passed more quickly than she had expected, and before she knew it, she was back in her own clothes, sipping a cappuccino and nibbling on a scone.

She flipped through the magazines on the table as she awaited the doctor's arrival. Emily practiced her deep breathing as her thoughts swirled around the possibility that he might come in and say the task was impossible. She jumped when the door clicked open and turned to meet the gaze of Dr. Dubois.

"*Bonjour*, Madame Emily. It is so nice to meet you. I trust that Giselle and Philippe treated you well?"

"Oh yes, doctor. They were very professional. Your staff

really is top-notch."

"*Très bien*. I am sure you must be very eager to see the results and a little anxious about this whole process," the doctor said as he walked over to the computer. "Please let me set your mind at ease." He tapped at the keys, and an image appeared on the screen. Emily was at a loss for words. Her very soul was enraptured by the beautiful woman on the screen."

"Who is that?"

"Why it is you, Madame Emily—or, more accurately, it will be you after our breakthrough treatment. Is it not to your satisfaction? Do you not look as you desired?"

"Oh goodness, yes. She is stunning. She is drop-dead gorgeous. Please don't toy with me. Those kinds of results are impossible."

"No, Emily. This is exactly how you will look. Our AI program is 99% accurate when depicting results. This truly is the wave of the future. Now shall we discuss the cost and our payment plans?"

"Yes, please do. I am very concerned now that a procedure of this magnitude will cost much more than I can afford."

"First, we require a down payment of $10,000. Is that manageable for you?"

"Yes. I can do that. I can clear out my savings for that."

"*Magnifique*! Our payment plans can then help you with the rest of the monetary cost. For most people, we can get it down to $200 a month for the next 36 months. Is that also manageable?"

"Seriously? That is all? I can afford that. Sign me up!"

"Well, that is not quite all. That is all for *monetary* considerations. There are a couple of other requirements that must be met, such as participation in future advertising campaigns. Shall we discuss that and the procedure itself?"

"Good point. I suppose I should understand what I am getting myself into here. Please proceed, Dr. Dubois."

Emily spent the next several hours deep in conversation with the doctor. She did have some reservations and concerns about the complicated process, but overall, she was eager to begin her journey of transformation.

Her mind made up, she went to the business office to apply for the payment plan, and was approved as expected. The doctor then sent her home with a large sheaf of documents to fill out while she waited during the required 48-hour holding period: Métamorphose did not allow their patients to make snap decisions about such a serious issue.

Emily only became surer that she wanted to proceed after her conversation with Allison that night. Allison mocked her confidence in the treatment's success. Even if she could've shown Allison the "after" pictures, she knew her friend would still doubt the veracity of their claims. All that mattered was that she managed to convince Allison to be her ride that day. She was determined to shut Allison's mouth for once and prove that she was not the know-it-all she believed herself to be.

Emily spent the next day filling out all the paperwork and then went to the bank to cash out her savings and obtain a cashier's check for the deposit to Métamorphose. The next morning, she jumped on the phone when it rang and was pleased to find Dr. Dubois on the line calling for her final decision.

"Yes, doctor. Thank you for calling. I have decided to proceed with the treatment plan. I will be by later this afternoon to drop off the deposit and my paperwork. My friend Allison has agreed to bring me the day of my procedure, so I just

# Shadow's Gate

need to schedule my appointment while I am there."

"*Très bien*, Emily. We will see you later today. *Adieu.*"

Emily couldn't wait any longer, so she drove off to the office as soon as she ended the call. Her procedure was scheduled for the end of the week because a cancellation had just come in. She called Allison on her way out the door to verify she would be available.

"Whatever, Em. I will see you Friday."

"Please promise me you won't tell anyone about my procedure or where you will be Friday."

"No problem. Trust me. I would much rather see everyone's reaction when they see you afterward. Mum's the word."

Friday came more quickly than expected. Emily was surprised to see that Allison actually arrived early to pick her up. Allison was notoriously late, so Emily had told her to arrive 15 minutes earlier than they actually needed to leave. Allison was only early because she had taken an Uber to Emily's house. She claimed that she was concerned Emily might get sick on the drive home and didn't want her car ruined. Emily didn't doubt that, but she also thought it likely that Allison was embarrassed that her car might be seen entering Métamorphose. She wanted people to believe her eternal youthfulness and beauty were all natural. Emily knew better: Genetics were a factor, but Allison had spent a fair amount of time under the knife as well.

Once again, Giselle greeted Emily at the door when they arrived at the clinic. Giselle thanked Allison for her selfless donation of time and caring to help her dear friend. Allison positively glowed at admiration and praise.

"We have a lovely convenience room for you to use while you wait for Emily's procedure to be finished. We have a wonderful selection of beverages, pastries, finger sandwiches and assorted delicacies for you to enjoy. Let me take you back there and get you situated, and then I will be back for Emily."

Allison nearly swooned with all the attention she was receiving. She followed Giselle back, beaming. Before Giselle could even return, Emily had already received a text with a selfie of Allison holding a cracker with caviar.

*Of course, this is all about you as usual, you selfish bitch.*

Emily looked up smiling when Giselle returned and led her back to pre-op. Dr. Dubois came in to say hi and get one last treatment authorization signed. He once again explained that they would be monitoring her vitals often since it was such a lengthy procedure. She would be given IV antibiotics before surgery, and blood would be on hand for transfusions if necessary. Emily said she understood and thanked him for his thoroughness. Dr. Dubois patted her hand before he walked away. At the door he turned and said, "Okay, Emily. I will see you in approximately six hours. Now, I must go attend to my other patient. Dr. Bouvier will be assisting me with both procedures today. Don't you worry now. I promise you will be very happy with the results."

Emily changed into a hospital gown, had her IV inserted and then was wheeled back to the OR. The surgical team greeted her and then asked her to slide over from the gurney to the operating table. The anesthesiologist placed an oxygen mask on her face as he said, "I need you to take slow, deep breaths. Count backwards from 10 please."

"10... 9... 8... 7..." Emily mumbled as her eyelids began to flutter.

Emily woke to the sound of people quietly talking somewhere across the room. Her eyes felt heavy as she strained

## Shadow's Gate

to open them. She moaned as her body began to stir. Her whole body felt as if it was on fire—the very air burning like acid.

"Don't move, sweetie. Everything is okay. I will let the doctor know you are awake. Andre is preparing some pain medication for you now."

"Was... was it successful?"

"The first part of the procedure went wonderfully. It is now time for your part. It is time for you to make that final decision. The doctor will be in shortly. Just relax for a moment."

"*Bonjour*, Emily. I see you are awake. Are you ready?"

"Yes, doctor."

"Andre is going to help you sit up now. You will find the mirror over here in front of the bed when you are prepared to look. When you are ready, Andre will help you—it is setting in your lap. Can you feel it? I will give you a few minutes."

Emily lifted her eyes so she could see herself in the mirror. She couldn't tear herself away from the sight before her. Tears welled up as she beheld the most beautiful woman she had ever seen, and she was that woman. She began sniffling as she cradled the object in her lap.

"Oh, Allison. It worked. Can you see? Can you see how beautiful I am? I am so sorry that I called you a bitch."

Allison did not respond. Emily continued, "I should have listened to you. You were right all along. My beauty is on the inside. Now you can see it on the outside."

Emily began to cry harder as she looked down. Tears streamed down her face as she cradled the suit on her lap. Allison's unseeing face stared up at her. She cradled to her chest the skin suit that was once Allison as she said, "I thought I wanted to look like you. You were the most beautiful woman to me. Everything came easy to you... friends, men, jobs and money.

# Sharon Marie Provost

I thought my life would be perfect if I was just like you, but I was wrong. I suppose you didn't deserve this end, but you must admit you were such a bitch. You thought I didn't hear the derogatory comments you made about me to others. You thought I was too stupid to understand that you made fun of me to my face."

Emily's body oozed bodily fluid and blood. Her muscles glistened and flexed as she adjusted her position on the table. Andre blotted her exposed muscles and tissues with gauze soaked in sterile saline to keep it viable. He squeezed ointment into her lidless eyes to moisten her eyeballs. Her abdomen and chest cavity were packed to protect her vital organs. When she paused speaking, he asked her, "Are you ready to put on the suit? It is time for you to decide if you want to switch to hers or return to your own. We cannot let these tissues dehydrate. We risk infection every moment we leave you exposed like this. The doctor needs to return the blood flow to one of these as soon as possible. The other needs to be put in saline in cold storage until the burn patient in OR3 is ready for the skin donation."

Emily looked up at Andre and nodded as she asked him to summon the doctor. Dr. Dubois returned, a quizzical look on his face, as he entered the room.

"Madame Emily, I am not sure I understand. I thought I would find you wearing one of the suits. We really must finish this procedure. Time is of the essence."

She held out her hands beckoning to herself as she stated, "I know, doctor. This is my decision. You can use both of these suits for other patients.. You can choose whichever one best matches the skin tone of the patient in the OR. Hopefully, you can call someone in on the waiting list that can make use of the other one as needed. I want to stay like this. My whole life, I have always been told that I am beautiful on the inside. Now I see it. I am finally happy."

Dr. Dubois pleaded with her, "Madame Emily, this is impossible. You cannot stay in this state. You will die... in a matter of hours, days at most. Your tissues will dry out and decay. You will develop a massive infection. Your pain level will quickly become unmanageable."

Emily lay back on the table, a wide smile on her face.

"I once saw a quote attributed to an unknown author. It stated *My growth came when I realized that I do not have to experience life the way I have been told to.* I finally understand now. Here, doctor. Take this to your next patient. Please leave me be. Let me experience life the way I want."

Dr. Dubois walked away, shaking his head. "*Oui, Madame.* What do you want us to do with the ashes from Madame Allison?" he asked as he paused at the door.

"She didn't suffer, did she?"

"*Non, mon cheri.* She was given an overdose of pentobarbital through her IV after we had finished harvesting. She never awoke from anesthesia."

"Good. Thank you for your compassion, doctor. Can someone spread her ashes somewhere in the forest surrounding the clinic? I think she would really like it there."

"*Oui, Madame.* Andre will see to your care and help control the pain. I must ask once more... are you sure?"

Emily laid her head back on the table and nodded, a serene smile on her face.

# Sharon Marie Provost

Shadow's Gate

# Poseidon's Revenge

"Why did you let those women aboard the ship? You doomed us."

"The HMS Trafalgar needed costly repairs before we could make our next voyage. Repairs that I could not afford. I charged that family a hefty toll to cross the sea given the risk we took by allowing them on the ship."

"If we allow them to keep taking up space, we face unimaginable peril.

# Sharon Marie Provost

*We barely survived the last storm. The ship has suffered more damage. Now there is a pestilence amongst the crew. Did you not see the red sky this morning? What further warning do we sailors need? We must throw them overboard, as soon as possible. You have their money; there is no further need to keep them on board."*

"I am an honorable man. We shall see what the weather brings today. That is my last word on this subject. You are a member of my crew, and you will do what I say."

"I hope you still have a crew to command by day's end."

Margaret and Edgar Bannister had a wonderful family with four beautiful daughters. The two raven-haired eldest, Matilda and Freya, aged 18 and 17, were quiet, studious girls. Both attracted many a boy to church to hear them sing in the choir. Their voices were likened to the tear-invoking virtuosos of the meadowlarks.

The flaxen-haired twins, Maisie and Amelia, age 15, were the adventurous, fun-loving members of the family, much like their mother. Most days, when they left school, they could be found on the shore playing in the surf, rather than collecting the promised mussels and clams they claimed as an excuse for being down there when one of their elder sisters came to reclaim them.

The family spent their evenings studying history. They especially loved the Greek mythological tales of Zeus and Hera, Aphrodite, Medusa, sirens, mermaids, Poseidon, Hades and the minotaur.

Edgar had left the family a little over a year ago to sail to America in search of a prosperous new life for them. Margaret had received a letter two weeks ago that it was finally time to bring the family over to settle.

# Shadow's Gate

She'd had an extremely difficult time finding a ship to book passage for five women. Sailors were a superstitious lot, and women were said to be bad luck on the open sea. But then Margaret learned of the HMS Trafalgar's financial difficulties, which made Captain Randall willing to take them on board... at a steep price. She gladly accepted the outrageous fares Captain Randall was charging and agreed to follow his rules of conduct to the letter in exchange for a private berth and safe passage for the family.

The stormy season drew nigh, but the ship had to undergo some repairs before crossing the Atlantic. The captain assured Margaret that they would safely make it across, so she set about tying up the family's affairs in Whitby.

The two oldest girls feared the crossing, but they were eager to settle in America and join the courting scene. The twins could barely control their enthusiasm and spent every day down by the dock watching the ship's repairs. But the weather began to worsen, and Margaret grew concerned they might not be able to set sail

The crew stepped up preparations, hoping to beat the coming storm. But in their hurry to prepare for the journey, no one had noticed that the maidenhead hadn't been restored to the bow of the ship after the completion of the repairs. Scylla, as they had named her, had always pleased the ocean Gods with her beauty, allowing them safe passage on calm seas.

Finally, one of the crewmen came by one day to announce that they would be setting sail on the morrow. The news allayed Margaret's fears concerning the weather since it had begun to change the past few days.

Things were looking up.

The family rose before dawn to meet the carriages that would carry them to the dock with all of their trunks. The awe-inspiring sight of the HMS Trafalgar as the first rays of dawn broke across it seemed to bode well for their journey. The crew eyed them suspiciously and with fear as they helped them board the ship. But Captain Randall greeted them kindly and showed them down to their berth. It would be a cramped journey for the next six weeks, but at least they were together.

The captain warned the family about the superstitious fears of the crew, and he asked them to be kind and respectful of the crew's wishes when it came to interacting with them. He told them to stay below decks whenever the seas were rough because it would be difficult, if not impossible, to rescue them should they fall overboard. The family would be served their meals in their berth.

Margaret and her daughters readily agreed to all his rules.

The captain took Margaret aside to warn her, "Do not leave the girls alone with any of my men, especially when they're below. I have warned them to leave all of you alone. But I cannot be held responsible if their longings for a woman's touch prompt them to do unseemly things with your beautiful girls."

The first week of the journey passed uneventfully as the skies lightened and the seas were calm. The tense atmosphere on the ship even started to ease.

Some of the younger sailors had taken a shine to the twins and their interest in the sailing, so they began to teach them how to man the rigging and sail the ship. Maisie took great delight in being allowed to steer the ship when Oscar was at the helm. Samual invited Amelia, accompanied by her mother, up on the deck at night so she could learn how to navigate by the stars. Matilda and Freya were still becoming accustomed to the ship's nausea-inducing rocking, so they spent hours sitting on deck watching the horizon and taking deep breaths of the ocean air.

Worries grew the following week as the seas rose and rolled the ship from side to side, hailing an approaching storm. The skies grew dark, and rain pounded the deck. The crew began to fear that they may have gone off course because they had not seen the stars in days to navigate by.

At midweek, they awoke to a red dawn and knew they were in for more trouble. The Bannister family was sent below and confined to their cabin. They were given some biscuits and a piece of salt pork to fend for themselves. The crew would be too busy to look after them.

Another storm came barreling in a few hours later. The family tried to hold on as they were tossed about the room. They could hear the worried voices of the crew as they shouted instructions back and forth. Water began to seep into the room from the flooded deck above.

"Mother, are we going to make it? Is the ship sinking?" asked Freya.

"Everything will be fine, my dears. Please don't worry. Climb up on your bunks and hold tight. Why don't you sing to pass the time?"

Margaret tried to appear as calm as the reassuring words she had just spoken. She sat on her own bunk and tried to darn a few of the girls' socks. The next seventeen hours felt like years, but slowly the storm died down—just in time it sounded like. The ship had made some alarming cracking sounds, followed by worried yells from the crew.

The girls had finally fallen asleep when the boat resumed its normal rocking, so Margaret crept up to the deck to survey the damage. The sail had been battered and torn by the wind before it could be taken down. Margaret offered to help sew up the tears, and the captain accepted with hearty appreciation. The crew was still working to bail water and repair damage to various parts of the ship, such as a small crack in the mast.

That repair work continued for the next two days. Maisie and Amelia offered to help the sailors with their work, while Matilda and Freya came up on deck to entertain the crew and make the long, back-breaking hours pass more quickly. Their crystal-clear voices soon drowned out the talking of the men. So entranced were they by the girls' charms, that the men became distracted from their work and sat down to listen to "the starlings," as they began to call them.

"What in the hell is going on here?" the second mate bellowed. "These repairs need to be completed today. The weather is only going to grow worse. Did I say you could sit on the job?"

With that, the trance was broken. The crew jumped up and resumed work, but their gaze drifted over to the two girls often, studying them closely, a hungry look in their eyes. This made the older girls uncomfortable, so they returned to their berth to read.

None of this escaped the second mate's notice.

He turned and stormed into the captain's cabin, intent on confronting the issue. "See, Captain! This is another reason not to have women aboard a ship. How can the men be expected to control themselves with four gorgeous young girls aboard? The twins are always distracting the younger sailors, feigning interest in their work. Then two of them start singing like angels straight out of Heaven's choir."

"Calm down now, Gregory! I will not say this again: You will leave those women alone. I will talk to them tonight and tell them to leave the sailors be and spend more time in their berth."

# Shadow's Gate

The following day, the family awoke to loud voices and the sounds of the crew bustling about. They learned that half the sailors had come down with a mysterious illness: They had developed a fever, muscle aches, loss of appetite, and abdominal pain. Some had even broken out in rashes. Captain Randall feared he had an epidemic of typhus on board, so he quarantined all the affected sailors belowdecks.

Once again, crew began to view the Bannisters with suspicion and fear. The girls heard the lieutenant and second mate speaking in hushed tones as the crew glared at them. Margaret began to worry that the crew was thinking about removing her family from the ship. However, the captain remained friendly and thanked her for fixing the sail. The family made sure to care for themselves and keep out of the way. Margaret, alone, went up to help care for the sick men on the deck.

The next morning, the skies dawned red as fire. As Margaret passed the captain's cabin on her way to her berth to retire after a long night of tending to the sick, she heard a cacophony of angry voices. It sounded as if the captain was having a heated discussion with some of the officers. Margaret crept closer to the cracked shutter to see if she could hear better: The officers were demanding that on she and her daughters be thrown overboard. They were convinced that the storms and disease were their punishment from having women on the open seas. The captain was still arguing on their behalf, but how much longer could he protect them before his crew mutinied?

Margaret kept her daughters down in the berth and out of sight of the crew. They ate the small number of biscuits and some beef that had been left over from the night before.

Late that afternoon, the seas became rough again as the

skies darkened. The menacing black clouds were a sure sign that another storm was coming in, and Margaret could only pray that this one wouldn't be too serious. The sail was once again taken down as the winds wailed around the ship like a banshee on the prowl.

As evening came on and the ship began to roll uncontrollably, the family heard the sound of feet stomping down the stairs. There was a sharp rap at the door, and then it was flung open. Margaret was greeted by the sight of the uncomfortable captain along with several of his officers. They charged in, grabbed the women and began dragging them up the stairs.

"I am so sorry, Mrs. Bannister," the captain said. "This was not my choice."

The girls were screaming and crying, begging for mercy, as they were dragged over to the railing.

"Please don't do this!" Maisie pleaded. "It is not our fault. We have helped you on this journey. If there is any reason for bad luck on this crossing, it is probably because the maidenhead is missing. Poseidon is not being soothed by her beauty, so he is not calming the seas," pleaded Maisie.

The crew appeared shocked as they looked over and realized the truth of her words. But instead of relenting, they blamed the oversight on the girls as well.

"I know what to do," the second mate yelled. "Let's throw the mom and the other three girls overboard. This little lassie must still have her maidenhead, so we will tie her to the bowsprit and make her the maidenhead for the Trafalgar. She is pretty enough to appease any god."

Several of the crew grabbed Maisie and began to strip off her clothes as she screamed and fought them. The second mate

# Shadow's Gate

punched her, knocking her out, so they didn't have to hear her screams. Before long, she was tied at the bow. Her body hung limply, sprayed by the cold ocean waves as the ship dipped and rolled on the high seas. Margaret and her daughters cried out as, one by one, they were picked up and tossed over the side of the ship.

Matilda and Freya, not being strong swimmers, began to flail and sink beneath the high waves. Margaret, a natural swimmer like the twins, worked with Amelia to keep the other two from drowning. But the storm continued to pelt the ship and the family, with no sign of letting up. The waves were so large that the family was dragged under with each one.

Eventually, the crew untied Maisie and dropped her into the sea, believing the gods were still unhappy. Having never regained consciousness, she slid beneath the waves. Amelia saw this and swam frantically to where her twin had fallen, leaving her mother to help her other sisters. She dove beneath the waves searching, but Maisie had disappeared in the murky depths.

The seas soon began to overtake the family as they tired from the effort to stay afloat. Matilda and Freya were lost next, drifting off and disappearing under the next volley of waves.

Eventually, even Amelia and Margaret, who had been clinging together, were torn asunder and taken by the sea.

The crew believed the storm lessened each time one of the women drowned. The crack in the mast worsened over the course of the storm, but it still held. When they no longer heard the cries of any of the women, the storm died down and drifted away. The sick crew collapsed from exhaustion after another night's long battle.

At first light, the crew was awakened by the cries of one of the sickest men, claiming he had seen a beautiful mermaid splashing in front of the bow. Those cries were followed by others who claimed to have seen two more mermaids: one to starboard and the other to port.

After a bit, the men grew tired and fell back into a deep slumber.

A few hours later, the crew awoke to the most beautiful song any of them had ever heard. They were entranced by two high-pitched, crystalline voices, filled with raw emotion, as if they were singing to God himself. All their attention was drawn to that song that somehow seemed so familiar. The ship was turned to find the source of their calls, but not one man could resist them.

They jumped overboard, desperate to find them.

Some of the men were good swimmers and headed off directly toward a rocky shore that had appeared before them. Others sank beneath the waves quickly.

The ship, drifting ever closer to shore without a crew to guide her, was soon dashed upon the shallow coral-laden depths.

Those men still swimming called out to the two beautiful girls perched on the rocks singing to them. Their heads and torsos were those of women, but they had the legs and wings of a giant bird.

Soon, the sailors realized there were three gorgeous mermaids swimming amongst them. The mermaids smiled and taunted them, popping in and out of the water at random. Or at least it seemed at random, until the men realized their numbers were dwindling. As a mermaid would disappear under the water, so did one of the men swimming toward the two sirens on shore. Before long, only the ruins of the ship attested to the fact that there had once been 50 men in that area.

The three mermaids returned to the shore, giggling, to greet the sirens.

"Oh dear, Momma, Daddy is going to be so lost without us," Freya cried.

"I know, my dears. But your daddy is a strong man. He will make it through. I am just so grateful we still have each other."

The mermaids climbed out of the water onto the rocks to sun themselves next to the sirens.

"Poseidon used the sea to punish those sailors for their transgressions, and we were transformed into the amazing creatures we are now," Margaret said. "We can live forever within Poseidon's kingdom and help him deliver punishment to those who do not respect him."

# Sharon Marie Provost

# Shadow's Gate

# Phrogger

The town of Lake Hiddenwaters, built around the south shore of the lake, consisted of a small gas station/mercantile, Bullfrog's Bar and Grill, a boat rental business connected with the resort on the southeastern side, and idyllic, private cabins deep in the woods on the north side. The so-called cabins, really more aptly described as medium-sized storybook homes straight out of a fairytale, were primarily used for Airbnb rentals by the wealthy.

Bullfrog's was popular with the resort crowd, with its garish neon lights and boldly colored sign depicting a large bullfrog hiccupping and belching "Howdy." People were drawn to quirky drink specials like Frog's Breath, a bright green cocktail made with Midori that emanated mist from the dry ice added, or Roadkill, a bright red and green cocktail made with melon liqueur and Advocaat.

Life was raucous and alcohol-fueled on the hard-partying south beach.

The homes on the north side were situated a mile apart from each other, close enough for occupants to interact with one another if desired, yet far enough apart that it was possible to never see your neighbor through the trees and thick underbrush.

The owners of those homes rarely used their own properties. They mostly rented them out to the privileged city dwellers who wanted to "glamp" while experiencing a bit of serene nature—complete with their nanny, housekeeper and personal chef.

This lifestyle made these rental properties ideal for Terrence.

Terrence had come up with his phrogging plan after watching a true crime show called *Phrogging: Hider in My House* on Lifetime. The phrogger lifestyle involved secretly living in someone's occupied house with them while avoiding detection. In theory, a phrogger should only take items that are absolutely necessary such as food or toiletries, while respecting the owner and their property. However, living in these houses with people of means gave Terrence the opportunity to take whatever he WANTED with impunity. The occupants neither noticed—nor cared, for that matter—when food or clothing disappeared. Even if it was noticed, it was blamed on the staff.

The homes were close enough that he could easily switch to another one if there were too many occupants to evade detection in the current one. Depending on the layout, he slept in closets, crawlspaces, or attics. He had even found a hidden

# Shadow's Gate

panic room in one cabin, and another, owned by the ultra-conservative, uber-religious CEO of an investment firm in the city, had a "den of iniquities" hidden behind a bookcase. It was obvious that he was a more frequent guest at his own cabin than the others, and most often *not* with his wife and children. Terrence had found that hidden gem by accident when he'd triggered a hidden switch while perusing the reading selection found on those shelves.

Terrence enjoyed a posh, albeit non-traditional, lifestyle. Even when he slept in one of the lushly carpeted closets or the attic, it was often more comfortable than the lumpy, sagging beds or couches he was accustomed to. Plus, he typically had his pick of 400-thread-count Egyptian cotton sheets, down comforters, and adjustable memory-foam pillows to make his own comfy nest.

Terrence had enjoyed foods he couldn't even pronounce and was hesitant to even consider what the ingredients might be for some of the exotic cuisine he encountered. He had never been one for high fashion, but he had begun to learn why some of those expensive designer outfits were sought after. They were made from the plushest fabrics, conformed comfortably to the body, and, most important, made him look as important as he felt.

*What the hell is wrong with me? I am living the life I have always dreamed of since I was a teenager. I haven't worked 9 to 5 in years. I have seen every movie and read every book that interests me. I soak in hot tubs, follow the latest skin care trends, eat to my heart's content. In fact, I should start watching those workout videos because I may have eaten too much. Why am I not happy? Why am I so bored? Dare I say it? Life is TOO easy! My very existence depends on being unseen... a shadow... But invisible is lonely.*

## Sharon Marie Provost

Terrence was so lost in his thoughts that he nearly missed the arrival of the latest tenant. As he scrambled to hide himself, the hatch to the attic squeaked before clicking into place after he retracted the stairs. He hurried across the floor beams, tripping over an old trunk, as he made his way to the window to see how many people had arrived. His brow furrowed as he bit his lip with bated breath, waiting to see if they had heard his flight out of sight.

"Roger, did you hear that?"

"Fuck yes, I did! With what I am paying per night for this place, there had better not be filthy vermin in this house. Where is Gerald? Is he still getting the bags for Christ's sake? Forget it! I will go upstairs and look."

Roger's feet thumping up the stairs announced his approach. Terrence retreated into the far side of the attic behind stacks of plastic storage tubs. He slid into the corner behind several large rolled up Persian rugs, out of sight unless someone moved them. Doors were slammed, one by one, as Roger checked out the second floor. Terrence knew this new arrival would not find any evidence of his presence because he was careful to always keep his belongings hidden well. Years of practice and an early near mishap had trained him never to leave items lying around unguarded.

On Terrence's second foray into the world of phrogging, he had set himself up in the home of a meticulous, clean freak... mistake one. He nearly got caught the first time he snuck down from the man's attic to eat because he didn't clean up all the breadcrumbs from his sandwich... mistake two. The man was uncanny about noticing the smallest change in his surroundings, let alone a mess in his spotless home.

The real problem occurred the day he spent watching

television in the man's living room. He was chilly because the house was kept at a nippy 60 degrees in winter, so he brought down his blanket. When he went outside to dispose of his trash before returning to his den, he accidentally left the blanket lying on the front porch. Terrence didn't realize his mistake until he heard the man calling his neighbors to ask them about it. Fortunately, a homeless man had been seen in the area recently raiding other neighbors' trashcans.

Still, Terrence had been forced to move out soon afterward because the man's security measures to protect his home became unmanageable.

The attic hatch was pulled down hard... the stairs slamming against the carpeted floor. Terrence could hear Roger's ragged, wheezing breaths as he hauled his considerable girth up the steps to peer inside. The effort to get up high enough to see in had apparently exhausted his energy because he retreated mere seconds after his head appeared and swiveled around in every direction. The hatch closed with a bang, and Terrence sighed in relief as he sank to the floor.

*Holy shit! That was a close one. I haven't been that scared in a... well uhm... now that I think about it... I haven't been that excited in years. It was exhilarating. The thrill of the pursuit. My potential discovery. That fucking rocked! That rich old slob was barely able to lift his own weight up those stairs. I bet his staff is going to hear it tonight for not being ready to cater to his every whim.*

Roger stomped down the stairs, slower than before, as he raged in between ragged breaths, "I don't see a goddamn thing up there. No signs of food scraps, torn bedding or droppings. It must have been the wind rattling the shutters or something. Has Gerald come in yet?"

# Sharon Marie Provost

"Yes, dear. He just carried the last of our bags into the master suite. He should be out any second."

Roger harrumphed as he settled into a dining room chair, mumbling, "We'll see."

"Did I hear you call me, Mr. Carlson? How may I assist you?" Gerald asked as he popped into the room as if by magic.

"Go upstairs and check the shutters on all the windows. One of them may be loose. There was some thumping upstairs as we arrived. I won't have that ruckus keeping me up all night."

"Very well, sir," Gerald replied as he bowed slightly before turning to walk out, pausing mid-step as Mr. Carlson began to speak again.

"You *had* to stay here, Audrey, in the middle of nowhere. Fifteen hundred dollars a night, and they can't even maintain the place. That sauna and hot tub better be in working order. I need to go relax."

Gerald followed Roger out of the room to prepare the sauna for him before heading upstairs. Audrey rolled her dark, unfeeling eyes as she sunk into the chair just vacated by her husband. "Ahhhh... that man drives me to drink," she grumbled as she leaned forward to examine the silver ice bucket holding a bottle of champagne with a satin bow around it. It had been calling to her from the middle of the table.

A small envelope leaned against it. She found a manila card inside written in impeccable calligraphy: *Bonjour! Welcome to your home away from home. Don't hesitate to contact us if you have any issues. Please enjoy this bottle of Dom Perignon with our compliments. You will find a platter with brie, gruyere, grapes, and foie gras in the refrigerator. In the breadbox, there is a fresh loaf of French bread flown in from the boulangerie in New York. Bon Appetit!*

"Mrs. Carlson, it has been a long trip. I am sure you must be

# Shadow's Gate

hungry. Would you like me to prepare you an early dinner?" Emily asked as she entered the kitchen.

"No. I am fine. There is a lovely charcuterie board in the refrigerator when I do feel like eating. Mr. Carlson is in one of his moods, so I am sure he will probably drink himself into a stupor before long. If you could just open this bottle of champagne, and then see to the unpacking and turn down the bed. That will be all, Emily, and then you can have the evening to do as you please."

"Thank you, Mrs. Carlson."

Audrey stood up and headed out to the veranda, calling back, "You can bring the bottle out here when you get it open."

Emily opened the bottle and poured some into a delicate crystal flute. She placed the bucket with the open bottle and the flute onto a silver serving tray and carried them out to Mrs. Carlson. There was a chill in the air, so she grabbed the cashmere throw blanket off the couch as she passed. She placed the blanket next to Mrs. Carlson on the chaise sofa before setting the tray on the coffee table. "Will there be anything else, Mrs. Carlson, before I prepare the room?" Emily asked as she turned to leave.

"No, Emily. Thank you. Have a good evening."

Emily walked into the house and was startled by a scuttling sound and a thunk from above.

*I hope Mr. Carlson was right about there not being any rodents here. I've got the creeps just thinking about it now. Wait... silly me! That is probably just Gerald upstairs checking the windows.*

She started forward again, not yet out of her reverie, and nearly ran into Gerald coming out of the exercise room, having just finished prepping the sauna for Mr. Carlson. She gasped before stammering, "Did... did you just hear that, Gerald? I thought it was you. Is someone else upstairs?"

"I didn't hear anything. Don't go getting carried away. It is a bit windy tonight. I will check everything out. You just get back to your work."

Emily turned away, cheeks burning, and headed up the stairs to the Carlsons' room. As she walked down the hall, she noticed the ceiling hatch appeared to be open a crack. She could have sworn it had been closed tight after Mr. Carlson came down, but maybe it had bounced back open given the way he slammed it shut. She proceeded into the room and performed the tasks without delay, anxious to have some time to herself as soon as possible. By the time she was finished, the tension had eased in her shoulders, and she bounced down the back stairs to her room in the corner.

Emily changed into jeans, a T-shirt, Vans sneakers, and then donned her warm, baggy NYU sweatshirt. She had unpacked her belongings as soon as they had arrived. She headed out the back door, determined to avoid the Carlsons—and therefore any chance of her time off being cut short—as well as Gerald's judgmental gaze. Her brisk step took her across the yard and down the path into the woods before Audrey could even shout to ask her for one more favor.

As the shadows of the large Sequoia trees deepened, she slowed her pace to enjoy the beauty surrounding her. A quick look at her phone confirmed her suspicion that if she kept close to the shore, her path would lead her directly to Bullfrog's patio in about three miles. Emily was in no hurry to return to the "Villa," as Audrey had decided to call it. With any luck, they would both have passed out in bed long before she returned that night. Gerald, ever the professional, would be ensconced in his room, ready to fulfill their every wish should they wake up.

# Shadow's Gate

Emily's long athletic frame allowed her to reached the bar and grill just as the sun began to drop in the sky. She chose a seat on the back of the deck near the water's edge: the perfect vantage point to enjoy the vibrant oranges and reds in the sky from the setting sun. She delighted in the delicious fried catfish, roasted garlic fingerling potatoes, grilled corn on the cob, and strawberry shortcake for dessert. She had a beer with dinner but finished off the evening with both of their signature froggy cocktails. By the time her evening was complete, she had completely forgotten her earlier anxiety.

A pleasant conversation with a young couple from NYC, sitting near her on the deck, also distracted her. She learned they had recently been married and were renting one of the homes nearby for their honeymoon. They were getting ready to go just as she was paying her bill, so they offered to give her a ride back to the other side of the lake. Emily graciously accepted because she was a bit tipsier than she had planned to be for such a long walk back in the dark.

On the ride back, Emily asked if they had experienced any unexplained noises or other issues at their rental. But all had been quiet at their place. The two of them giggled as the woman, Clarissa, explained their only mishap during the trip.

"We had ordered a dinner in from Bullfrog's, and it had just been delivered. I set it all out on the patio table. Mark came up behind me and kissed me on the neck. One thing led to another—we are newlyweds after all—and we ran down to the lake to skinny dip. Sometime later, when we emerged from the water, our clothes were strewn about, some of them... well some of Mark's were missing, and our food had disappeared from the table. This is an active forest—we have seen raccoons, opossums, deer, squirrel, rabbits and foxes—so we assumed that one of them had absconded with his clothes for their den and enjoyed our lovely food."

Mark laughed at his wife's candid account of their exploits. When he saw the concerned look on Emily's face, he questioned, "Why do you ask? Have you had any problems at your place? You said you just arrived today, right?"

"My employer and his wife heard some weird noises when we first arrived, but he couldn't find a cause. Then I heard them again later. I suppose they could just be wildlife on the roof, but yet... somehow, they just sounded too... too premeditated... too deliberate. I must sound crazy. Never mind. Forget I brought it up. I grew up in New York City. I am probably too suspicious by nature."

Mark and Clarissa smiled and laughed with her. Clarissa pointed out their adorable cottage that looked like it was straight out of Hansel and Gretel, only missing the gumdrops and peppermints plastered to the walls. They were only a mile away to the northeast of the Carlsons' rental. As they dropped her at the house, Mark said, "You are welcome to come over to visit whenever you like, if you get some free time again."

Clarissa giggled and winked as she amended his statement, "Well you are welcome *almost* any time, but if the cottage is a rockin', don't come a knockin'."

Emily got out of the car, laughing and shaking her head. "Thank you very much for the entertaining company tonight. I hope you enjoy the rest of your honeymoon."

Clarissa's giggle devolved into a cackle as Mark peeled away from the curb, his arm wrapped tightly around her shoulders. Emily headed into the house through the back door again, locking it for the night behind her. Most of the lights were off, and the house was still. She took a quick peek into the kitchen and, as she expected, it appeared undisturbed. She

# Shadow's Gate

tiptoed down the hall past Gerald's room and into her own. Emily turned the handle as she pushed the door closed so it would not click into place announcing her return. Only then did she turn on the light as she turned to face her bed.

Astonishment and anger rushed across her face in a reddish-purple flush on her cheeks. *What the actual fuck? Who the fuck thinks they have the right to go through my belongings? And then to not even put them away after they got their rocks off spying on me. I put their fucking shit away discreetly.*

Emily's hands thunked inside the dresser drawers as she flung her clothes back into them before slamming them shut again. Someone had even gone through her toiletries caddy, and her expensive shampoo was missing. Emily never wasted money on buying brand name makeup and fancy soaps, but it was a different story when it came to her unruly, curly mop. This was the only shampoo she had ever found that could tame her wild 'do. There was little to no chance she would find more in that tiny excuse for a store in the mercantile on the other side of the lake. Now she would have to order it online and pay for expedited shipping. She flopped on the bed, fuming, as she realized that she dare not ask the Carlsons or Gerald about it because they would take it as an accusation... which it was, if she was honest about it.

A quiet but insistent knock at her bedroom door made her jump. She opened it and found the normally pale-faced Gerald purple with rage, staring down his hawkish nose at her as he spat his words, "What exactly is going on here, Miss Jones? Do you know what time it is? The Carlsons have retired for the night. You are going to wake them with all the noise you are making in here. Mrs. Carlson was nice enough to give you the night off, and this is how you repay her kindness. You young people these days are a disgrace!"

Emily bowed her head, her face flushing red with embarrassment; the wind taken completely out of her sails.

*Why is it that this man can make me feel like a petulant child again? I have a right to be upset.*

"I apologize, Gerald. I was upset because I found that someone had rifled through and removed all my clothing and toiletries from their place in the dresser. It was an invasion of my privacy... a breach of my trust. I just don't understand why they would do this. There's something else... something was miss..."

"Stop right there before you finish that statement! You do not want to go there. The outfit Mrs. Carlson was wearing today cost more than your salary for the past year. They have no need to take anything you might have. You have chosen to live in their household. They must have had good reason to search your belongings. It is not for you to question, Miss Jones. Now go to bed, and do not make any further noises to disturb this household. I will see you in the morning bright and early. Mr. Carlson has a business meeting via Zoom at 6 a.m. Mrs. Carlson wants to do yoga at sunrise. You will need to have their breakfast ready and be prepared to fulfill whatever needs they may have otherwise. I will be busy with the plans for the small soiree they want to throw for business associates this weekend."

Emily plugged her phone in and set her alarm for 5 a.m. She crawled into bed, feeling too frustrated to sleep, but was too exhausted not to drop off soon after her head hit the pillow. A few hours later, in the pale moonlight filtering through her window, she awoke to a noise in the corner of her room. Her exhaustion overwhelmed her, but as she struggled to open her

# Shadow's Gate

eyes, she could have sworn she saw a shadow cross the room and slip out her door in near silence. Her pulse pounded in the vein on her forehead as her heart raced. She finally managed to open her eyes completely and flicked on the bedside light to find nothing and no one. She laid her head back on the pillow and resolved to go back to sleep after her nightmare.

The next morning, Emily rose groggy, a pounding headache throbbing in her temples. She reached into her dresser to pull out some clothes. As her eyes rose, she was shocked to see her shampoo sitting there on the top of the dresser next to her toiletries caddy. Her heart leapt into her throat.

*Someone was in my room last night. It wasn't a nightmare after all! But then again, I did have quite a few drinks last night. Could I have missed it? I was pretty pissed seeing all my stuff laid out. No, goddamnit! It wasn't fucking here. I am not imagining this shit. Well, there is no sense debating this now. I don't have time.*

Emily finished getting ready and headed out to the kitchen. She started heating the water for Mr. Carlson's soft-boiled eggs while she began cutting up Mrs. Carlson's fruit plate and making her toast. Not surprisingly, Gerald showed up to check on her, but he left without a word when he saw she had everything under control. She was just setting the food out on the table when Mr. Carlson whisked into the room, already on a conference call. He grabbed his coffee cup off the table and motioned for her to bring the food back to his office. She heard Mrs. Carlson coming down the stairs as she followed him back.

When she returned, Mrs. Carlson was sitting at the table, head in her hands, clearly feeling the effects of that large bottle of champagne. Her normally perfectly coiffed platinum blonde hair was loosely pulled into a ponytail. Mrs. Carlson always looked ready to hit the red carpet, but today she was wearing a

Juicy Couture velour tracksuit. Emily had thought ahead and prepared her favorite hangover-cure smoothie and placed two aspirins next to the glass. Mrs. Carlson had already started on those.

"Would you carry my breakfast out to the veranda and set up my yoga mat and music? I will be out there in a moment," Mrs. Carlson said as she walked out of the kitchen, smoothie in hand.

Emily retrieved the yoga mat and then carried it out with the food. Luckily, she had remembered to connect her phone to the house Wi-Fi yesterday, so she was able to quickly connect to the whole home audio system. She brought up Mrs. Carlson's yoga playlist on Pandora and set it to play on the speakers outside. Now she had a little free time to prepare for the rest of the day's activities and look over her room for more signs of tampering. She finished cleaning the kitchen and then turned to head down the hallway.

"Oh, Emily. I forgot to mention that my friend will be coming in from the city around 1 o'clock. We will be having a late lunch in the sitting room. I never ate last night, so you can just serve that charcuterie board. Please make us some of your delicious lemonade as well."

"Yes, Mrs. Carlson. Are you going to be staying here for the visit, or will you need me to drive you two somewhere?"

"I am not sure at this point. She hasn't decided how long her visit will be yet. If she stays for dinner, we will probably just have Gerald drive us into Emoryville to the French restaurant there. I will let you know if you need to prepare a room for her to stay the night. Otherwise, you may have to see to Roger's needs depending on his work schedule."

"Yes, Mrs. Carlson. I am going to run over to the mercantile to grab some items, so I am prepared for however the day goes. I will go see if Mr. Carlson is off his conference call yet in case he needs something."

Emily stopped by Roger's office on her way to her room. She could still hear him on the phone. She sent him a text message asking if he needed her to run any errands for him and his plans for the evening. She took her time investigating her room and found nothing else out of place. She still hadn't decided whether to broach the subject with the Carlsons. She had worked for them for five years now, and they had never done something like this before, not even when she first started. Nothing had changed lately to make them lose faith in her, so she just couldn't understand why they had breached her privacy in such a blatant way.

She checked her phone and found that Mr. Carlson had finally answered her. He would be busy working most of the day. He requested that she make him steak frites with hollandaise sauce and serve it at 6 p.m. during a short break in his schedule. Otherwise, he did not want to be disturbed. Emily jotted down a quick grocery list and headed out to the car. She narrowly dodged a run-in with Gerald by slipping out the side door when she heard his voice approaching.

Fighting her own headache, Emily was grateful to get out of the house and have some peace and quiet for a while. Her schedule was pretty tight, but she took her time shopping at the mercantile. She was surprised to find almost all of the ingredients without incident and even adequate substitutes for the rest. She returned to the house feeling relaxed and at ease. However, she walked in to find a raging Mrs. Carlson.

"Finally! There she is! We will take care of this issue now," she heard Gerald say in his clipped tone as he rushed toward her as she opened the door.

"Miss Jones, did Mrs. Carlson not explicitly tell you that she and her friend would be dining on that charcuterie board for lunch this afternoon? How could you think you had a right to eat any of that in the first place, let alone after she told you that?"

"Excuse me. I don't understand."

"I was quite clear. I spoke to you in English. How exactly did you think you had a right to partake of any of that food when you knew she wanted to serve it for lunch?"

"Yes, she did say she was going to eat that for lunch. Is it not in the refrigerator? I saw it there, looking pristine, I might add, when I made their breakfast this morning. It was still there untouched when I cleaned the kitchen and left for the store. I just got home. I haven't touched it at all… ever."

"Follow me, Miss Jones. Explain this to me then," Gerald growled as he grabbed her arm, leading her into the kitchen. The platter sat on the kitchen counter, over half the food eaten. Large chunks had been cut out of the brie and gruyere cheeses. The foie gras had been almost completely consumed and looked as if someone had just dipped crackers directly into it. Half the grapes had been plucked from the stems. The loaf of French bread had been cut into rough pieces directly on the countertop spreading crumbs across it, and it had been left open to dry out.

"You think I did that? Never! I haven't even been home. I just bought all these groceries."

"Well Mrs. Carlson certainly did not do that. She asked Mr. Carlson, and he had not touched it either. As I told you I would be last night, I have been out making plans for the soiree this weekend. I just arrived home five minutes ago. You were here for some time after you served Mrs. Carlson breakfast, before you left for the store. What were you doing?"

# Shadow's Gate

"I was checking my room over while I waited for an answer from Mr. Carlson. You said I needed to be ready to attend to their needs. I had to find out if he had any errands for me and if he needed dinner tonight."

Mrs. Carlson entered the room, glaring at Emily as she spat, "Checking your room for what exactly? Gerald told me about your accusations. How dare you! Roger and I have every right to search your belongings any time we want. You live under our roof. However, we have not touched your things. We certainly did not steal your precious bottle of cheap shampoo. I wouldn't be caught dead using that. I buy my beauty supplies directly from Roberto. You know that!"

"Yes, ma'am. I..."

"Don't you dare ma'am me, you ingrate!"

"Mrs. Carlson, I apologize. My mother raised me to always be polite. I am happy to hear that you didn't start doubting my loyalty and search my room. I just couldn't understand. But don't you see? If you didn't search my room, then who did? Someone is coming into the house. That must be the cause of the noises. And they must have eaten the food."

"That is patently ridiculous. How would they be getting in and out of the house without any of us seeing them? Besides, we are not living in a slum. That kind of thing doesn't happen here. You are skating on thin ice here. We don't have time to keep discussing this farcical story of yours. I need you to go back to the store and come up with something to replace this food you have eaten. If you can admit your wrongdoing and keep me from being embarrassed during this visit, I will let this all go."

Tears streaming down her face, Emily put the groceries away and packaged up the leftover food. Then she turned and left for the mercantile again, racking her brain for what menu would impress Mrs. Carlson's friend. Emily's feelings flipped from fear of losing her job to fear of the identity and motives of the unknown intruder entering the house to anger over not being believed. She didn't know how she was going to handle this situation, except make sure the house was kept locked up tonight. Right at this moment though, she knew she needed to focus on saving her job.

Emily returned from the store and began to make cucumber sandwiches. She had not noticed earlier, but the mercantile had a small fine food section catering to the rich clientele that frequented the area. She was able to replace the foie gras and brie and substitute camembert for the gruyere, and she found some delicate French crackers. The grape selection was not up to Mrs. Carlson's standards, which is why she had decided to make the sandwiches. She washed the tray and quickly placed all the items on it—in fact, it looked better than the original tray had.

She had just finished the lemonade and was carrying the food out to the veranda when Mrs. Carlson's friend arrived. She rushed to the door to greet her and ushered her outside. Mrs. Carlson stepped through the French doors just as Buffy Sinclair exclaimed, "Oh, how wonderful! What a delicious feast she has prepared for us."

"Yes, Mrs. Sinclair. Mrs. Carlson is a wonder, isn't she? Oh, here she is now. I will leave you two alone, unless you need anything," Emily inquired with an eyebrow raised.

"That will be all, Emily."

Emily returned to the kitchen to finish cleaning up. She had a few hours to catch up on some work and social media posts Mrs. Carlson had asked her to make this week before she needed to start Mr. Carlson's dinner. First, she made her way around the house making sure that all the doors and windows

# Shadow's Gate

were locked, except for the French doors out to the veranda and the front door that Gerald was using.

At 3 p.m., there was a knock at her bedroom door. Gerald sneered as he informed her, "I will be taking Mrs. Carlson and her guest into Emoryville. They will be doing some shopping and getting drinks before their dinner reservation at 8 p.m. We will be getting home quite late, so make sure to attend to any needs Mr. Carlson may have. Prepare the guest room on the second floor for Mrs. Sinclair. You will find her bag downstairs in the foyer. Make sure you stay out of trouble tonight."

"Yes, Gerald. I am just attending to some duties Mrs. Carlson has assigned me, and then I will be making Mr. Carlson's dinner at the appointed time. He has asked to be left alone otherwise, but he knows he can reach me by text should he need me. I will just be sitting in the living room reading tonight once I finish my work. I shall attend to the room now."

Gerald turned on his heel without acknowledging her answer; the slam of the front door the punctuation to his utter disregard for her feelings. Emily retrieved Mrs. Sinclair's overnight bag and took it up to the guest room. She placed fresh towels and soap in the en suite bathroom, turned down the bedcovers, and placed a mint on the pillow. She unloaded her suitcase into the bureau next to the bed and hung her clothes in the closet. Then she placed her beauty supplies on the vanity across the room before stowing the suitcase in the closet. She had opened the window to let in fresh air as she worked but was careful to close it again before exiting.

Upon returning to the lower level, she proceeded to lock the front door and the door out to the veranda. It was nearing 5, so she returned to her room to finish her work before she started dinner in about 30 minutes. When she was done, she took the completed documents up to Mrs. Carlson's desk in her room. When she came back downstairs, she found the French doors to veranda standing open.

*Mr. Carlson must have gone out for a bit of fresh air before his dinner.*

The breeze felt good, so she left them open as she proceeded into the kitchen.

She peeled and chopped the potatoes and started the sauce first. Mr. Carlson liked his steak rare, so she began cooking it as she put the potatoes on to fry. As she dropped the last of the fries in the oil, she heard the French doors close and heavy footsteps going up the stairs. She hoped Mr. Carlson wouldn't be too long, because his dinner was nearly complete. A few minutes later, as she plated his dinner and opened a bottle of red wine and placed it on the tray with a wine glass, she heard the click of a door down the hall. She thought it odd that she hadn't heard his thundering footfalls coming down the stairs, but she had been singing along to music from the '80s.

She proceeded to his office and knocked on the door, which swung open at her touch. Mr. Carlson was not seated at his desk or elsewhere in the room. As she turned around to look down the hall, she nearly dropped the tray when she started as she backed up into him.

"Miss Jones, are you okay?"

"Yes, sir. I apologize. I heard you go outside and then upstairs a little while ago. Then I heard your office door just a moment ago and thought you had returned. It just scared me when I backed up into you."

"No harm, no foul, Miss Jones. I just left the office to use the restroom. I haven't been upstairs in quite a while."

"Are you saying you did not go outside and then upstairs about 10 minutes ago?"

"Miss Jones, I have heard about your irrational fears. I really don't know what is going on with you. And to be honest, I really don't have time for all these questions. Can you just please serve me my dinner and let me return to work?"

"Yes, sir. I apologize," she murmured as she placed the tray on the coffee table by the couch. She poured him a glass of wine before placing his plate and the bottle on the table. 'Will there be anything else, sir?"

"No, that is all. You look tired. Maybe you should turn in early after you clean up the kitchen. Perhaps that will help resolve this anxiety of yours. I would really hate to lose you as an employee after five faithful years of service."

"I may do that, sir. My phone will be on. Just call or text me should you need anything."

Emily tried to calm her nerves. *He is a busy man. He has been working all day with no break. Perhaps, he simply lost track of time. He must have been the one who went outside.*

Emily checked the French doors and found them securely closed and locked. Then she headed upstairs to look for anything amiss. All of the rooms looked just as she had last seen them... all except for the mint missing from Mrs. Sinclair's pillow. *That man is a candy fiend. He must have spied it as he walked past to his bedroom. Like a small child, or in this case one very large child, he can't even leave one piece of chocolate alone.* She replaced the candy before returning to the kitchen to eat her dinner and finish cleaning.

Emily retrieved the sandwich she had picked up from the deli in the mercantile and sat down at the kitchen table, reading her book as she ate. After she had finished, she washed all the dishes and cleaned the countertops. Ready to return to her room, she turned to pick up her phone from the ledge by the stove but couldn't find it. She patted all her pockets and searched every nook and cranny in the kitchen before retracing her steps throughout the house. It was nowhere to be found.

She returned to her room and flopped on her bed in disgust. She felt a hard object pressing into her lower back as she lay there. She got up and found her phone lying in the center of the bed. She certainly had not been in her room since before dinnertime. The last time she had seen her phone she had paused the music when she went to serve Mr. Carlson.

*Someone moved my phone. There is someone in the house!*

Emily jumped up from the bed. She crept down the hall to Mr. Carlson's office, and she could hear him on a call or Zoom meeting with multiple people.

*He will fire me for sure if I disturb him. He is in his office and connected to multiple people live right. He should be safe. I need to resolve this issue now... and on my own.*

She jumped when she heard a loud click and then some shuffling noises from upstairs.

*Maybe I can catch sight of him from outside. Hell! I am safer outside right now if he is inside anyhow.*

She sprinted on tiptoe across the living room and opened the French doors, careful not to make a sound. She crept out onto the veranda and slipped down the stairs. Looking up, she saw a light on in one of the upstairs rooms.

A shadow passed by the window.

Shocked, she jumped backward and tripped over a rock in the garden, landing with a thud and a loud "Oof!"

A face appeared in the window looking out toward where she lay in the garden. She held her breath and body still, hoping she couldn't be seen in the darkness.

*That was not Mr. Carlson!*

When he pulled back from the window, she jumped again

# Shadow's Gate

and ran through the shadows in the yard cast by the tall Sequoias. It was a moonlit night, and she needed to avoid the bright, open areas. She rounded the corner of the house and made a break across the yard to hide behind the shed at the edge of the forest, praying that she had not been seen.

She fished through her pockets trying to remember which one she had stuffed her cell phone into moments ago. Finally, she found it, but her frantic movements didn't seem to be working to unlock her phone. In fact, nothing she did even made the screen light up at all. Her phone had been acting up lately, and sometimes, if she reset the battery, it worked. She leaned out into the light a fraction, trying to find the cover that let her access the battery.

The darkness above and around her deepened as she heard a deep voice ask, "Are you looking for this?"

Her eyes rolled up to see her phone's battery in a hand looming over her shoulder. She opened her mouth to scream just as his other hand clamped over it... tight.

"If you scream, I will hurt you. Do you understand?"

Emily nodded. He slowly released pressure from her mouth. She turned to look at the owner of the voice as she asked, "Why are you terrorizing me?"

He smiled as he replied, "Because you are the one who knew I was home with you."

Near midnight, Gerald pulled into the driveway and let Mrs. Carlson and Mrs. Sinclair off at the door before returning the car to the garage. They walked up the steps and entered the unlocked front door. The house was darkened and quiet. To Mrs. Carlson's relief, everything appeared to be tidy and in order. As she showed Mrs. Sinclair to her room, she bid her goodnight. "I trust that everything is in order for you, but if you need anything you can reach Emily on her cell. Here is the number. I had a wonderful day with you. Thank you for coming to visit."

Mr. Carlson rose early for another long day of work. He did not expect to see his wife or their guest until late morning given the late hour of their return. He was not pleased when he went down to get his morning coffee and found the kitchen dark and still. He had expected that Gerald would be gone early because he had sent him into the city on some errands. However, Miss Jones knew he was working early all week and expected his soft-boiled eggs. He was running late and didn't have time to track her down, so as he proceeded to his office, he sent her an angry text message asking her to explain herself.

He slammed the door behind him when an urgent call came in from his COO. There was a problem at the office, and he completely lost track of time. When he hung up the phone, he didn't realize how much time had passed until the growling of his stomach was drowned out by his wife's angry voice upstairs. Nearly two hours had gone by since he had texted her.

*This has really gone too far. I hate to lose a good employee, but this girl needs some help.*

He swung open his office door and turned the corner tight, almost knocking down Audrey as he did. She was enraged, and he shrank back against the wall.

*No need to poke that bear.*

"Where in the hell is Emily? I need to find that girl *now*."

"I haven't seen her all morning. My breakfast was not prepared. The kitchen was dark. Have you checked her room?"

"I was just headed there when you almost ran into me. Oh, Emily unloaded Buffy's suitcase all right… into her own room, presumably. Buffy is missing her vintage 6-carat diamond tennis

# Shadow's Gate

bracelet. We scoured that room. It was not put into any of the drawers, on the vanity or dropped underneath the bed. It was not lost in the lining of the suitcase. It is gone. This is outrageous! I am livid... livid I tell you!"

"Just relax, darling. We will find it. We will handle this situation. Let's find her and see what she has to say for herself."

The Carlsons proceeded to Emily's room in the back corner. Audrey didn't bother to knock, just swung the door open with a bang... to an empty room. Emily's bed had either been made or never slept in. All her belongings were still in their place, including her purse and car keys, but there was no sight of her or her phone. There was no note explaining her absence, either.

"She must be around here somewhere."

"She must be on the lam. Someone could have picked her up."

Roger rolled his eyes as he said, "Yes, I suppose. But that doesn't seem logical now, does it? Who would leave their purse and identification? She left all her personal belongings behind, including her laptop and those family photos. Those are all she has left of her family. She would never leave those behind."

"Maybe it didn't seem so important compared to a $12,000 bracelet. She has been acting erratic. She is probably on drugs."

"I agree she has been a little paranoid and not her normal self, but I think that may be a bit of a stretch. Let's search this room and make sure the bracelet isn't here. If she hasn't returned by the time we are done and Gerald returns, we will call the police to report the missing bracelet and the mysterious circumstances surrounding her. Agreed?"

"Fine. But in the meantime, she does not have her keys to get into this house, so I am locking it up tight now. She will have to ring that doorbell and face us directly to gain entry. And I am going to pack up her belongings and hide them. I will not leave them where she can find a way to sneak in and retrieve them."

Gerald searched the room thoroughly as he packed Emily's personal items into her suitcases. He could hear Audrey's screeching voice as she proceeded through the house, making sure all the doors and windows were locked. Gerald found nothing to explain Emily's behavior, nor any items that did not belong to her. He found Audrey sitting at the kitchen table with Buffy, apologizing to her for the missing bracelet.

Buffy exuded an air of haughty indignation as she listened to Audrey. Her nose held high, a faux tone of sympathy and judgment in her voice, as she said, "Well, I have never experienced this before. Chip and I have always vetted our staff with a comprehensive background check, required letters of recommendation from reliable sources, and they must have a minimum of 10 years of experience. I would have had my driver accompany me and drive me home last night, even if our visit had run late, if I had known this was going to happen. I am truly just appalled. You know that bracelet is an antique. It is absolutely irreplaceable."

"I promise you that we will prosecute her to the fullest extent of the law. We will be contacting the police as soon as Gerald returns if he does not know Miss Jones' location. We will do whatever we have to in order to find her... and your bracelet. I will get a private investigator on the case *today*."

"I really have no desire to stay here any longer. I have packed up my suitcase. If you could take it to the car, Roger, I will be on my way immediately. I wish I could say that I enjoyed this visit." Within seconds, the house was still, but the anger and anxiety were palpable. Gerald pulled into the drive seconds after Buffy Sinclair rounded the curve out of sight. Audrey

# Shadow's Gate

rushed to the car, assailing him with questions, "Where is Miss Jones now? Why wasn't she here this morning? Did she take Mrs. Sinclair's bracelet? Answer me!"

Gerald frowned and looked confused at the questions. "I'm sorry. How should I know Miss Jones' location? After getting to bed after midnight last night, I was up at 4 a.m. this morning driving to the city to complete some urgent business matters for Mr. Carlson. No one had risen yet when I left the house. The last time I saw Miss Jones was just before we left yesterday afternoon. And what is this about a bracelet?"

Roger stepped forward explaining the situation in detail. Gerald's face was grim but betrayed his triumph. "I told you I did not trust that girl, Mrs. Carlson. I never have! I thought we should have let her go the other day after her accusation. Have you called the police?"

The Carlsons looked at each other and shook their heads.

"I will get to that right now. Should I contact Mr. Howards at Eye-Q? I think we should learn more about that girl's background and see if he can find any leads as to her location."

"That would be wonderful, Gerald. I appreciate your faithful service. I need to get back to work right now. I will try to clear my schedule for the afternoon, so that I can deal with the police when they arrive."

Audrey pursed her lips, biting her tongue... for once. Gerald led Mrs. Carlson back inside and started making calls. He placed a delivery order at Bullfrog's for his employers' breakfast first. As he was talking to Mr. Howards, he made some coffee and delivered steaming cups to both of them. The police were out on a call involving a large accident on the highway just outside of town. They promised to be there in the next couple of hours.

The arrival of the police car drew the attention of more

than a couple of neighbors. They might be out of sight of each other, but word traveled fast. Lake Hiddenwaters had no need for the Nextdoor app. The police were there for over an hour, and speculation ranged from a domestic to murder-suicide and even to embezzlement or money laundering. Audrey was well-known in the area for her hot temper and vociferous complaints. Likewise, some of Roger's business exploits had raised more than a few questions.

Audrey flew to the door when she heard a tentative knock shortly after the detectives' departure. The report had been filed, but she didn't know what good it would do. The police had not seemed convinced that Emily was a thief and appeared to be more concerned about her whereabouts. Not that they would pursue that matter, though, since she had only been missing for slightly over 12 hours.

*Maybe that hesitant knock is a contrite Emily back to confess and beg for mercy for the error of her ways. Stupid girl! Fast track to jail is more like it.*

"Uhh... hello," Clarissa stammered as she stared at the disgusted, disappointed face of Mrs. Carlson.

"We don't want any. Did you not see the private property sign? We don't deal with solicitors," Audrey snapped as she started to close the door.

"Ma'am, we are not selling anything. My wife and I are staying at the next house over. She was concerned, well we both were, when we saw the police car here. We just wanted to make sure everyone was okay. We met Emily a couple of nights ago when we dined at Bullfrog's. She had expressed some concern about some strange noises at the house. She asked if we had experienced anything odd. We told her about someone absconding with our dinner and some of my clothes lying on the

# Shadow's Gate

beach. That someone probably being a raccoon, that is."

"Oh, so you know Emily? Come in, please."

"Well, no, not really. We just met her for the first time the other night. We had a pleasant evening of conversation out on the deck as we all enjoyed dinner and cocktails. She just seemed so worried the other night. I probably let my imagination run away with me, like Mark always tells me. I wanted to check in though."

"I wouldn't be too concerned, at least not about your safety. Roger and I do not believe there is any intruder to be concerned about. However, I wouldn't trust my valuables around Emily. She is a troubled girl who comes from a difficult past. We called the police because my friend was visiting, and her very expensive bracelet turned up missing. Miss Jones did not show up this morning to perform her assigned duties. Don't get me wrong. I don't think anything bad happened to her. However, her behavior on this trip has been very erratic, so I am concerned that she may have a substance abuse issue."

"Oh, I see. I am very sorry to hear that. If we hear from her, we will let you know. I apologize for the intrusion, ma'am," Mark said as he extended his hand.

Audrey did not shake his hand, instead just draping her fingers in his, almost as if he should kiss her hand like she was some old Hollywood starlet or royalty. Mark awkwardly tightened his fingers around hers and then let go, draping his arm around Clarissa as he turned to walk her home.

Clarissa's worried eyes met his as they reached the end of the drive.

"I know, sweetheart," he whispered as he leaned forward to place a kiss on her forehead.

"I don't believe any of that about Emily. Something is not

right there."

She shivered in his arms, even though the day was warm, and the shadows had been chased away by the bright sunlight streaming through the trees. She hastened her pace, eager to be out of the open and once again safely locked inside their delightful cottage. She couldn't help but look back over her shoulder, feeling eyes on them from someone hidden in the shadows deep in the forest behind them. That feeling followed them all the way back and pervaded their once happy home.

Audrey closed the door hard, frustrated at the lack of progress. She couldn't leave the hard feelings between her and one of her oldest and dearest friends—she'd known Buffy since they joined society 30 years ago when Roger hit it big on the stock market.

She called out to Gerald: "Gerald, please ready the car. I need you to take me into the city. I must see Buffy right away. Let Mr. Carlson know that we will be gone most of the day."

Audrey trotted up the stairs to retrieve her handbag. As she passed the guest room, she wondered why Roger had closed the door or whether the police had done so after searching it. She continued into their room and was angry when she saw the way they had shuffled through their drawers. The drawers had been left open, and the clothes were in disarray. The closet was open, and the clothes had been haphazardly shoved to the side.

*What exactly were they looking for? We were the ones who called to report the crime. What right do they have to search our bedroom and treat our belongings with such disregard? The contents of those drawers and the closet were worth more than what the two of them earned in a year... put together.*

Audrey searched for her laptop, but she couldn't find it

anywhere.

*Roger is probably using it downstairs. I don't know why he bought that expensive desktop computer when all he ever wants to use is my laptop. I don't have time for this right now. I can just use my phone. But so help me, he better give it back to me tomorrow.*

She turned on her heel and met Gerald waiting for her at the bottom of the stairs.

"Mr. Carlson is just finishing up a phone call out on the porch. He wanted to say goodbye. I will go get the car and meet you out front shortly."

Audrey walked out onto the porch just as Roger hung up. He smiled at her and said, "Please don't worry, darling. We will get this all worked out. We will find that bracelet, and all will be well with Buffy once again. Why don't you spend the night in the city and try to relax? I have quite a bit of work later this afternoon and evening. Then I will have a few days of free time, so we can enjoy our time here. I will see you tomorrow at lunch. Okay?"

Audrey nodded with tight lips and turned to walk down to the car as Gerald pulled up. Roger followed and climbed into the back seat with her.

"Gerald, drop me off at the mercantile on your way out. I need a bit of fresh air before I jump onto that next Zoom conference. I am going to grab something easy for dinner and then walk back."

"Yes, sir."

"Did you lock the door, Roger? I don't want that girl getting back in there and stealing our stuff?"

"Yes, of course I did. Gerald locked the French doors when you were upstairs. See... front door locked now," Roger said as he punched the lock button on the Smart Home app on his phone.

Roger picked up a six-pack of beer and a slice of cheesecake at the store. Then he walked across to Bullfrog's to place a delivery order for dinner—16-ounce T-Bone steak, twice-baked potatoes and corn on the cob—Audrey would kill him if she knew he was eating this way. He walked back to the house, pleased with his temporary coup; he had the house to himself, a delicious dinner on the way at 6, dessert, and beer. He cut through the woods to save a little distance, entering the house through the side door closest to his office.

He closed the door quietly, entranced by the rare moment of silence. As he turned to enter his office, he heard footsteps and then a squeaking sound, followed by a thump upstairs. *How did she get in here? She left her keys behind. And I talked to the homeowners and had them change the passcode to the app so she couldn't use the keyless entry.*

Roger ascended the stairs slowly, careful not to betray his presence. He checked each room one by one, looking under beds, in closets and behind doors, but there was no one to be found. The windows were even locked, so she couldn't have slipped out of one of them. As he walked back down the hallway to go downstairs, he noticed the hatch to the attic was not closed tightly.

*Damn it! How stupid am I? I forgot about the attic. She has probably been hiding up there the whole time. She never left at all!*

Roger pulled on the cord to open the hatch and extend the fold-up stairs. He climbed up the stairs and peered into the attic. The stacks of plastic storage containers had been moved, creating more of a wall, to obscure the view... but of what? Hoisting himself up with some effort, he walked across the

# Shadow's Gate

attic, and as he got closer, he caught sight of what appeared to be the top of Emily's head.

"I see you back there. There is no sense hiding anymore. Just come out, and we can talk about this."

His statement was met with silence.

He continued forward and, as he rounded the corner of the wall, he was confronted with Emily's pale, lifeless body. Her throat had been slit, the Garfield shirt she had been wearing in the evening now soaked crimson with her blood. A knife protruded from her chest. Roger stumbled backwards, struggling to process what he was seeing.

A voice emanated from the darkness in the corner. "I didn't realize you had returned home. I was nearly finished. Two minutes longer, and it would never have come to this."

A figure stepped out from behind the stacks of rolled Persian rugs tucked there. "I guess we are going to have to figure out what to do with you."

Terrence reached down, roughly pulling the large chef's knife out of Emily's chest, as he stepped toward Roger.

Roger backed away, tripping over a beam in his haste. His voice croaked as he begged for his life. "Don't be so hasty. We can work this out. I have money... a lot of money. We can both walk out of here safe and happy. I will pay you whatever you ask. I won't call the cops. No one will ever know what happened here."

"It is a little late for that. The cops have already been called and been out here at the house. I have enjoyed my stay here. Now you have jeopardized all that I have worked for the last few years. The homeowners have already been alerted to an issue. They may think it is regarding Miss Jones over there, but they are likely to increase security now. That threatens my livelihood. Someone needs to pay for that. I think that someone is *you.*"

Roger turned to run, but his bulky frame was neither fast nor agile. In one quick movement, Terrence lurched forward, wrapping his arm around Roger's neck, slicing across his throat from one ear to the other. The edges gaped open like a grotesque mouth vomiting an endless stream of blood. Roger gurgled as blood filled his lungs and oozed from his mouth as he sank into Terrence's arms, looking up one final time.

*Well, it looks like it was a good idea that I took that young man's clothes off the beach. I am going to need a change of outfit after this.*

Terrence climbed down the fold-up stairs and went to the utility closet to obtain some cleaning supplies. Then he returned to the attic and wrapped Roger in a tarp he had stashed there after retrieving it from the backyard shed. He dragged Roger's body behind the wall of containers, placing it beside Emily's. Then he began the laborious task of cleaning up all signs that an attack had occurred there. Afterward, he finished the task he had been working on earlier and further built up the wall that hid the bodies from sight. He left only a slight cleft in the back that would allow him to slip through the wall and conceal himself behind the rugs.

*Two more people to go, and then I just need to dispose of the bodies and the car containing their belongings where they will never be seen again. Then I can clean up the house and take a hiatus from here. Lay low for a while in one of the others.*

Terrence heard the doorbell ring below. He peeked carefully out of the attic window and saw the contactless delivery of Roger's food on the porch.

*Perfect! I have quite an appetite after all that work.*

Terrence waited a couple of moments, then darted out to grab the bag. He flopped down on the couch, grateful to have a comfortable place to enjoy his food without having to hurry. He savored every moment of his recent victory as he did each bite of that steak.

*I should go check on that couple later. They were a little too suspicious for my comfort. I could have sworn her eyes were boring into me, like she was looking right at me, but she couldn't possibly have seen me.*

Terrence disposed of the trash and went in search of Roger's phone. To his surprise, it had not been on him when he ventured into the attic earlier. Terrence found it on the center of his desk. He sent a quick text message to Audrey to explain Roger's absence when she returned home in the morning: *I know I promised my work would be completed by the time you returned, so we could spend some time together. One last issue has come up. The quickest way for me to resolve it is to run into the city and see to it personally. I will be home well before dinner, and then I am all yours.*

A short text message was received in return. *Typical! We shall see.* Terrence muted the phone's volume and pocketed it.

Terrence spent the afternoon and early evening watching cable television while he partook of Roger's beer and cheesecake. When the last vestiges of twilight had faded, he ventured out into the forest to spy on that couple. A couple of hours later, he returned, exhausted after a long, hard day and retired to the Carlsons' bedroom for a restful night's sleep.

The day dawned bright and sunny much earlier than he would have liked. He had much to prepare before Audrey's arrival. He made the bed and placed Audrey's missing laptop on the center of the bed. He double-checked the room before his departure to remove any signs that a stranger had been there. Then he went down to the living room and kitchen to clean up the trash from the night before and carry it out to the cans at the street. He knew Roger always hid any signs of his improper diet. Then he went to the router and disconnected it, disabling the Wi-Fi.

Terrence enjoyed his lifestyle because he was able to avoid interactions with people. He had learned that one could be an extrovert but still find most people deplorable or boring. Rarely did he meet someone whose company he enjoyed. He found that he was really quite looking forward to making Gerald and Audrey suffer. He found them both utterly despicable and cruel, and was convinced the world would be better off without them.

He was just about to sit down and relax for a bit when he heard a car pull up outside. He looked out to see Audrey and Gerald arriving home earlier than expected.

He climbed into the cupboard under the stairs in the hallway, so he could hear their plans.

Audrey came in complaining about seemingly everything. Gerald followed close behind carrying her bags, which he dropped off in her room. As he descended the stairs, he told her, "I will be back shortly. I am going to pick up some necessities at the mercantile and place your delivery order at Bullfrog's for tonight."

When Audrey went upstairs to unpack, Terrence climbed out of the cupboard. On the way to the side door, he opened the door to Emily's room, letting it bounce off the doorstop, and left her cell phone sitting on the bedside table.

Audrey walked to the head of the stairs and called down, "Gerald, is that you? I thought you were going to the store."

She was greeted with silence.

"Roger?"

Terrence backed out of the room and headed down to the garage to await Gerald's return, letting the outside door click shut behind him. Audrey descended the stairs to see if Roger had arrived home earlier than expected.

She turned down the hallway to his office and saw that Emily's room was open at the end of the hall. She rushed down, intent on catching her in the act of home invasion, only to find an empty room. Well, not totally empty, as her eyes came to rest on Emily's phone.

*Damn it! That little bitch had the audacity to come back here and sneak in. The stupid gutter snipe forgot her phone this time, and she is not getting it back.*

Audrey rushed to the side door to see if Emily was in sight, but there was no one around. She locked the door and put Emily's phone in her pocket as she dug out her own. She closed Emily's door as she dialed. As she walked to the front door to lock it, she talked to the police, letting them know that Emily was not missing as they had feared and had instead just "broken into" her home. They told her to call back if Emily returned.

*This is way too much for my poor nerves! I need a mimosa.*

Audrey walked into the kitchen and opened the refrigerator to get the champagne and orange juice. She noticed various food items were missing.

*Roger never makes food for himself. How long has that girl been around here? Was Roger even here last night?*

She prepared her drink and then took it to the couch, grabbing her book on the way. She placed her cell phone on the coffee table before reclining on the couch intent on enjoying her book and calming her nerves.

Terrence heard a car coming up the drive, so he backed into the shadows beside a large cupboard built around the water heater.

Gerald backed the car in and came around to remove the

groceries from the trunk. He was focused on a message he was reading on his cell phone, so he never noticed the dark shape that darted at him. He started when the arm wrapped around his neck, covering his mouth, but he didn't have time to react before the needle sank into his jugular.

He struggled to free himself for the next 30 seconds before the effects of the succinylcholine—a skeletal muscle relaxant that inhibited neuromuscular transmission—began to take hold. Gerald began to have difficulty moving at all, and he couldn't seem to draw a breath: his diaphragm was affected as well. He was still conscious and could feel the painful grip around his neck—the burning in his lungs as they cried out for air—but he couldn't move.

For the next 60 seconds, his mind ran a million miles an hour, desperate for a way to get some oxygen, but his chest would not expand. Before long, oxygen deprivation took over, and his conscious mind sank into blackness.

Terrence stood over Gerald for the next ten minutes, then checked for a pulse that was no longer there. He dragged his body over to the water heater closet and stowed it in there for now.

*Fuck! That was exciting! It was all I expected and more. It is amazing what one can buy online if you have the right contacts. One more to go—and this one should be the most fun yet.*

Terrence stowed the groceries Gerald had bought in the bushes near the side door before he crept up the back stairs to the veranda and peered inside. Audrey was there in the living room, drinking and reading. He crept back down and went around to the side. She had locked the door, but he used Roger's phone to access the Smart Home app to unlock it again. He

## Shadow's Gate

walked down the hall and crossed over to the kitchen, groceries in hand.

Audrey's head bobbed down a little; she appeared to be falling asleep. Terrence removed the champagne and orange juice from the countertop and placed them back into the refrigerator. He placed the bag of groceries on the table and unlocked the front door.

He heard Audrey begin to stir in the next room, so he slipped out the front door and around to the side porch, out of sight.

Audrey woke from her light sleep when her book dropped out of her hands into her lap. She set the book down on the coffee table and walked up the stairs to use the restroom.

Terrence saw her go up the stairs through the window on the side door. He used this opportunity to place a surprise in Emily's room for Audrey to find later. Then he hid behind the bedroom door when he heard Audrey come back down the stairs and cross over to the kitchen before slipping out the side door again.

Mystified, Audrey walked over to the bag on the table and looked inside to find groceries.

*Gerald must have gotten back. But why didn't he put away the groceries? Maybe he is getting another bag from the car.*

Audrey returned to her primary mission of refilling her mimosa but was interrupted by a knock at the door. She opened the door to find a young man standing there.

"Excuse me, ma'am. Is Emily here?"

Audrey's face screwed up in disgust, her anger apparent. "No, she most definitely is not! She does not live here. Who, may I ask, are you?"

"Sorry to disturb you, ma'am," the young man mumbled as he turned and walked away.

Audrey slammed the door and stalked into the kitchen intent on fixing her drink. She couldn't find the champagne and orange juice where she had left them on the table, so she walked back over to the fridge and opened it. There they were, inside. Perplexed, but more irritated than anything, she snatched them off the shelf and stomped back into the living room.

She set her drink on the coffee table and reached out for her phone to search for a replacement assistant and houseworker.

But it wasn't there.

*I could have sworn I put it on the table. It was right here.*

Audrey got up and began to search in the living room and kitchen, but the missing phone was nowhere to be found.

*Maybe I took it upstairs earlier. If nothing else, I saw Roger left my laptop on the bed.*

Audrey went upstairs and, after a few minutes of searching fruitlessly for the phone, returned with her laptop instead.

She settled into the couch once more and powered up her laptop as she took a long drink of her mimosa. She typed in Google, but was met with an error message: "Unable to connect to the Internet." She tried to connect to the Wi-Fi, but to no avail.

*What the fuck else can go wrong today?*

She slammed her laptop on the coffee table just as she heard another knock at the door. She stood up and stomped back over to answer it.

She opened the door to find the same young man standing there. Anger and sarcasm dripping in her voice, she said, "What do you want now?"

"Is Emily here?" he asked once again.

# Shadow's Gate

"Are you a simpleton? I told you no."

"Are you sure?"

Audrey's face bloomed purple with rage as she slammed the door. She crossed the living room in a few angry steps and flew out the back door onto the veranda to get some fresh air.

*If that asshole knocks on the door one more time, I will call the police.*

As Audrey paced back and forth, Terrence entered the front door and went upstairs to hide while he waited. *It is only a matter of time before that statement gets to her. She will check... soon.*

Audrey calmed down after a while and sat down on the couch again. She downed her drink in one swallow.

*Where the hell is Roger? I thought he would be here by now.*

She reached for her phone again to call him and slammed her hand on the table when it occurred to her that she had not found it yet. She tried to reconnect to the Wi-Fi so she could email him, but it still wasn't working.

Then she remembered that she had Emily's phone in her pocket.

*Yes! I do have a connection to the outside world.*

She pulled the phone out and pressed the button to wake it up. No response. She tried pressing the power button, but it would not turn on. As she threw it on the table, it occurred to her that it felt a little light in her hand. She picked it back up and opened the back to find that the battery was missing.

*Now that is strange. Why would Emily remove the battery? Why would she sneak in and leave it here for me to find?*

Audrey leaned over, head in her hands, frustrated by all the mysteries around her. Frustrated that she couldn't call Roger. Wondering where Gerald went. Wondering who that strange young man was and why he came back again to ask if she was sure that Emily wasn't here.

*Oh, my God!* "Are you sure?" he asked. *My God, is she still here?*

Audrey jumped up and ran back to Emily's room. She was certain she had closed the door earlier after finding the phone, but there it was, open again. Her step slowed as she approached the door. As she crossed the threshold, a scream built up in her throat when she saw those vacant eyes staring at her. When she touched Gerald's cold, lifeless body, the scream finally erupted from her throat. The sound of her pulse pounding in her ears and her own ragged breaths as she hyperventilated were all she could hear... at first. Then she heard a thump from upstairs and the sound of someone walking down the stairs.

Audrey came to her senses and bolted out the side door. She tore across the yard and into the forest, unsure where to run. Audrey did yoga, but she was far from fit. She needed to find help or someplace to hide—and fast. Then it occurred to her: That young couple from the other day said they were staying in the next house over. A mile. She only needed to make it one mile. She hazarded a glance over her shoulder, and was thankful she did not see anybody behind her. Yet.

Audrey thundered up the steps and grabbed the handle to the front door. It turned. It was unlocked! She slammed the door behind her and locked it, screaming out for help. There was no response. There had been a car out front, so they must be around somewhere. She ran through the house, searching each room as she went. The last door that led to the master bedroom was shut.

*Newlyweds! That's right. They must be in there.*

Audrey burst into the room and found them in bed, as she had expected. What she didn't expect was to find them in *that state*. They were lying there, unclothed, hands and feet tied. They had been bludgeoned to death by a hammer, which was still laying on the bed. The young woman's skull was caved in on the right side. Her cheekbone and eye socket on that side were smashed. Her eye—what was left of it—protruded from the socket. The body of the young man was unrecognizable; a mass of torn flesh, broken bone and blood.

Audrey ran back out to the kitchen and picked up the phone... no dial tone. She ran to the front window to look at the car and realized the tires had been flattened. She needed to run to the next house for help.

*One mile! Just one more mile!*

Audrey wrenched open the back door and ran out, stopping dead, a loud "Ooomph" passing from her lips. Her wide eyes looked down to see a large chef's knife protruding from her chest. She tried in vain to take a breath as her lung collapsed. Terrence smiled as he pulled the knife out and then stabbed it into her abdomen just below her sternum. He laughed as he drew the blade down, disemboweling her. Blood poured from the gaping maw as loops of bowel slithered out, splattering onto the deck. She collapsed to her knees with a thud. A barely audible wheeze passed her lips as she mouthed, "Why?"

"Because you were there... destroying the peace of my home."

Audrey slumped to the ground as her breathing ceased. Terrence dragged her body back into the house and then closed the door. Now the painstaking process of cleanup.

He walked to the garage and opened it to reveal Mark's diesel truck with a Tonneau cover over the bed. He drove the truck over to the Carlsons to begin there. He spent the next day packing up everything that belonged to them. He removed all the food in the house and disposed of it. Then he loaded the bodies into the bed of the truck along with their possessions. It took him another full day to remove all traces of blood from the house with repeated bleach washes. He wiped down every surface where he might have left his fingerprints. Then he loaded those cleaning supplies into another duffel bag. The home looked even more immaculate than it had been before the Carlsons rented it.

Then he drove over to the young couple's home and repeated the process. When it was complete, he loaded rocks into the duffel bag full of bloody rags.

During the years he had spent living in the area, he had discovered the perfect place to dispose of their bodies, possessions and cars where they would never be found: an open-pit copper mine dug in the early 20$^{th}$ century about five miles from the town. The 800-foot-deep pit had filled up with groundwater over the years, forming a toxic lake filled with the by-products from the ore processing, including arsenic, cadmium, and lead, among other toxins. The bodies and all the rest would be covered with more than 450 feet of murky, dark green toxic water. He pushed the other cars loaded with the suitcases over first. Then he stabbed each of the bodies in the lungs, so they would sink, before pushing the truck containing them over the edge as well.

Terrence started the long walk home. He decided it may be a good idea to lay low for a while. There are plenty of homes available in the area in which he could live. When he got back to the housing development, he collected his belongings from the bushes where he had stashed them. He walked through the forest, investigating all the nearby homes. He knew he had found his next abode when he came across a French-style

# Shadow's Gate

Storybook home with a tower containing a leaded glass window. He waited until dark to do further reconnaissance, verifying that it was currently unoccupied.

Terrence fell in love with this new home. It had a variety of interesting hiding places, including a basement, an understairs cupboard, a secret crawlspace that led from the closet of one of the smaller bedrooms into the lower floor of the tower, and even a small unfinished attic under the tower's pitched roof.

He had settled in for only a week when the first renters showed up. Terrence had set himself up in the unfinished attic, prepared for just this moment. As he peered through the tower window, watching them come in with their staff, he realized they had an inquisitive young boy with them.

Terrence sighed. *I hope I am not going to have an issue again.*

# Sharon Marie Provost

# Hell's Bell

Mortecai hated the graveyard shift. It was cold, dark, and to be honest, goddamn spooky. It was bad enough that he spent every night cleaning up the cemetery and digging graves for services the following day. But it was beyond morbid to sit graveside all night every time someone was buried, waiting for a dead ringer. Besides, had anyone ever actually been buried alive and then saved by ringing a bell? Nobody in the village had ever heard of such a thing.

But he was new in town, and had to take whatever work he could get. So, here he was, sitting graveside for a man that no one in town even knew.

The man, now christened Unknown for eternity, had been found lifeless... and nearly bloodless, in the woods on the outskirts of Edenburgh. Mr. Edwards had been traveling in his wagon after picking up more supplies for his mercantile when he saw someone lying in the woods. He ran out to help the man, thinking it might be Old Man Withers, when he found it was a stranger instead. Good Christian man that he was, he loaded the body into the wagon and drove his team hard to Doc Summers, just in case he wasn't beyond help.

Doc had taken one look at the man and pronounced him dead on the spot. Word spread through the village regarding the man's pallor, and his pronounced veins from the desiccation. People began to worry that he had brought disease with him.

Doc tried to allay everyone's fears, but he couldn't adequately explain the man's pale complexion without letting them know about his exsanguination from unknown causes. The villagers were scared enough without stirring up their superstitious tendencies. To be honest, Doc was mystified by the pair of puncture wounds found near the man's collarbone. He listed the official cause of death as a copperhead snakebite.

Mortecai had seen the state of the man's body that evening when he helped prepare him for burial. No man could possibly rise again looking like that. Besides, he was cold and stiff. Yet, he had been tasked with tying a bell to the man's finger and leading the cord up through the coffin before lashing it to a bell hung on a stake next to the grave. Only then was he allowed to fill the grave and place the small wooden headstone that simply read, "Unknown RIP."

Mortecai had been provided with a bucket to attend to his needs; he'd been given some hardtack to snack on and a blanket to keep warm. As he saw it, that just wasn't good enough. A bitter wind had begun to blow small snowflakes through the air.

*No one cares about poor, little old Mortecai. They are too busy looking at me with derision or suspicion. What did I ever do to them? They never gave me a chance. What harm could there be if I just went over there to the edge of the woods? A little windbreak... I could make myself a small fire—I would still be within earshot. I could be back in place before the sun rises, and no one would be the wiser.*

Mortecai gathered his supplies and moved under the branches of a large oak tree. There was a small pile of branches a short distance away that he had collected earlier when cleaning up the cemetery. He'd been planning to take them home for his hearth, but realized he would be much better served if he made use of them now. Before long, he was sitting by a small but welcoming fire, snuggled under his blanket, as he ate his hardtack.

As his eyes began to drift closed, he heard a small tinkling from the bell. He eyed it suspiciously, but soon realized the tinkling occurred every time a large gust of wind came up. He checked the cord, and there was no tension on it from below. He once again settled down by his fire, determined to be diligent and stay awake.

However, his exhaustion soon overtook his good intentions once again. The moon had risen high in the sky when Mortecai was roused from sleep once more. His mind slowly swam to consciousness to the beat of a jaunty Irish jig—ringing out on a bell. His head snapped to the right to see the bell... the only bell in the area, ringing in time to the tune; there was no longer any wind blowing to explain the movement. Mortecai sprang to his feet and ran over to the gravesite. He pulled up several times on the now-taut cord as he leaned over and bellowed, "Hello! Rap on the wood if you are alive in there."

Mortecai thought he heard a low cackle as a subtle rapping began below him. He raced over to the equipment shed to grab his shovel. As he approached the grave, he realized the rapping had become thunderous crashing, followed by the sound of wood splintering. He backed away from the grave, shaking his head in denial. Then, with one last *bang*, the ground opened up and the deceased man sprang from the grave... very much alive... a wicked grin upon his face exposing two long, sharp fangs.

Mortecai turned to run for his life; he knew a vampire when he saw one. His left leg was stretched out to take the next long stride when he felt an arm wrap around his chest from behind. He was pulled backward—his body pressed tight against the vampire as he felt the man's lips and then teeth upon his neck. The vampire whispered into his ear menacingly, "Don't fight me, or you will be sorry. My name is O'Malley. And who might you be?"

"My... my... my name is Mortecai. I am the grave digger and caretaker here."

"And here would be?"

"You are in Edenburgh. Edwards found you just outside of the village in the forest."

"Ahh, that makes sense. I was in Ashbury and headed here to do some business."

"H...h...how did you come to be in your current state?"

"A vampire you mean? I was a day's ride outside of town

and had just settled down for the night when I was accosted. A vampire drained me of blood until I was barely conscious, and then he gave me a choice. He could leave me there to die, or I could partake of his blood and be granted eternal life myself. It really wasn't a choice to me. I am not ready to die... now... or ever."

"So, what happened after you drank his blood?"

"I was so delirious and weak. He explained that I would die in the next few hours. The change doesn't occur until after you've been buried in the ground. He put me on my horse and spurred him down the road. I really had no idea what direction he had sent me."

"Are you going to kill me?"

"I am tempted. I should... he told me I would need to feed a lot as soon as I rose. I am utterly famished. But I was once an honorable man. You were out here watching over my grave, so I will let you go... at least for now. First, you must promise, though." O'Malley released his grip on Mortecai and turned him around to stare into his eyes.

"Anything. What do I need to promise?"

"You can never tell anybody about what you saw here tonight. I need you to re-cover my gravesite, so it looks undisturbed. There will be deaths tonight, but you must feign ignorance."

Mortecai readily agreed, grabbing his shovel and throwing the dirt back into the grave as fast as he could. "So be it! As you wish. I would never say anything. I don't care about any of these selfish, ignorant people. They will find me here in the morning performing my appointed duty, watching over your grave."

"I don't think I shall feast on you then."

"Can I ask you something?"

"I suppose. I may not answer it, but we shall see."

"Why did you play that tune with the bell?"

"It scared the wits of you, did it not? I woke up gloriously happy... all my experiences are so much more intense now. I wanted to have some fun."

Mortecai threw another shovelful of dirt into the grave before turning back toward the vampire to ask, "Is this another game? Are you lying to me now about not killing me?"

In the blink of an eye, O'Malley had disappeared from sight; only his parting statement lingered in the air, "Farewell, Mortecai. Remember your promise."

Mortecai resumed his work of refilling the empty gravesite. When he was done, not even he could tell it had ever been reopened. He returned to his seat at the campfire and pretended to watch over the grave once more. Over the course of the night, he ignored the faint screams he heard echoing through the darkness. The repercussions of his promise to O'Malley would be dealt with soon enough when the morning dawned. He would be spending another long night tomorrow beside several new graves.

Just before dawn, he was relieved by the daytime caretaker. He walked home and dropped into bed, bone tired, as soon as he arrived. He was roused from his sleep hours later, as the sun was setting, by a large mob of villagers carrying torches.

"Come out of there now, Mortecai! We have your lair surrounded. There is no escape."

Then another, more authoritative voice said, "Oh, Henry! Stop with the theatrics. Mortecai, we need you to let us in and answer some questions."

Mortecai sprang from his bed. He was still dressed from last night. As he opened the door, Henry Mullins pushed his way in, followed by the constable and William Edgerton. A

# Shadow's Gate

large crowd of people seemed to be milling around nearby. Mortecai invited them to have a seat at his dining table, as he asked, "So constable, what is this all about? You just roused me, so I am not sure what's going on here."

"I need you to tell me your whereabouts last night."

"I am sure you know that I work at the cemetery. I was on dead ringer watch for that stranger who was buried there yesterday."

"Yes, you were seen there by multiple witnesses in the evening. However, Mr. Atkins told us you were missing after 3 a.m. when he and his son returned home after helping with the calving at the widow Nathan's house."

"I was too cold in the wind and the snow last night. I moved over to the edge of the woods and started a small fire where I could still see and hear any noises coming from the gravesite. I never left the cemetery all night until I was relieved by Mr. Waters, just before sunup."

"Did you see the Atkins go by last night? Did you see anyone else in the area? Any suspicious activity?"

"No, I didn't see anybody. To be honest, I accidentally fell asleep around 2 a.m. for a couple of hours. Can I ask what all of this is about? What happened last night?"

"Three villagers were found dead, with their throats ripped out."

"Who?"

"You must have seen the assailant pass by on his travels between the MacGregors' and the Sanders' farms. I just don't believe you about falling asleep. It is a little too convenient that, on the night of these horrific murders, you were not only missing from your post but asleep and ignorant of the madness that ensued. You must have heard the screams. No one could have slept through that."

"I understand your suspicion, but that is what happened."

"This is your last chance to tell me the truth, Mortecai. If you are covering up for someone, it is time for you to speak up... for your own sake. If you did it, it will go better for you if you admit it. I don't know how much longer I can control that crowd out there."

Mortecai's brow furrowed with concern. He was scared of what the crowd might do, but he was terrified of the vampire. He had to keep his promise. He stammered, "I wish... I wish I could help you, but I really don't know anything. I admit I shouldn't have wandered from my post, but I could see and hear if anything had happened at the grave. I regret falling asleep, but it was a quiet night. Well, I mean... it was quiet there."

"I see. Henry... William... it is time."

Multiple hands were gripping Mortecai's arms before he even realized it was happening. His hands were tied together, and then he was dragged through town to the small church that doubled as a courthouse. Except this didn't feel like he was going to be put on trial; mob mentality had taken over, and vigilante justice was the order of the day. He was placed in a chair at the front of the church, where he could see all the villagers streaming in the door, glaring at him.

The constable moved to the lectern at the front of the church, his face beet red and the veins in his forehead throbbing as he glared down at Mortecai, seated in front of him. "Mortecai Wallace, you stand accused of vampirism. You are never seen in the light of day. You dwell in the nighttime hours, when the forces of darkness reign. Doc Summers admitted that he falsified the cause of death of the stranger found yesterday. He was found devoid of blood with twin puncture wounds on his neck.

# Shadow's Gate

"Last night, it was your job to sit by his graveside to watch over the bell. Two villagers reported that you were missing for hours last night. During that time, three villagers, including Mrs. MacGregor and her daughter, as well as Mr. Sanders, were drained of their blood horrifically. Their throats were literally torn out in your feeding frenzy!

"We questioned you earlier about two witness reports of your absence from the cemetery during the hours the murders occurred. Your claim to have been sitting at the edge of the forest can't be verified by any independent witnesses. Frankly, I just don't find it believable. None of us do. I know for a fact you have been on dead ringer watch many a cold night this winter, and you have never left your post to start a fire. What do you say to these charges?"

"This is outrageous! I plead innocent, of course. I have never hurt anybody in my life. I was right there in the cemetery all night. I swear!

"You are a newcomer to this area. We never had any strange deaths before your arrival. Then you showed up in July, and a few weeks later, we started hearing reports of missing people in the woods between here and Ashbury, Terwilliger, and Willowgate. That seems like too much of a coincidence to me."

"Look there! The blood on his clothes," came a cry from the crowd in the church.

"How do you explain that, Mortecai?"

"I was involved in the preparation of the unknown man for burial yesterday."

"But we know he was found bloodless. We told you that. I think it is time for a vote. All those who find him guilty and sentence him to death, say Aye."

A chorus of "Ayes" was heard throughout the church.

"Any nays?"

The room was silent as everyone looked around the room to see if anyone would dare vote to save the sadistic interloper's life. Mortecai was grabbed roughly and iron chains put on his wrists. The burly men in town picked him up and carried him out into the courtyard in the center of town. The manacles were removed just long enough to secure him in the stocks, then reapplied.

The constable approached him with a sharpened wooden stake as Father Donahue prayed for his soul.

Mortecai begged for his life, "Wait! Wait please, I beg of you. It was not me. I didn't kill those villagers. You are right. There is a vampire here, but it is not me. Last night as I watched over the unknown grave, he rose again. He made me promise not to tell, or he would have killed me. I can help you search for him, and then you will see. We can rid the village of this pestilence! If you don't listen to me, more people will die."

A loud cry arose from the crowd, "Kill him. Bring the stake! Bring the stake!"

When the prayer was finished, the constable placed the stake against his chest and hammered it into his heart. Mortecai's scream was cut off as blood gurgled in his throat, running out of the corner of his mouth to join the flood pumping out of his chest. A few seconds later, his body slumped, supported only by his hands and neck locked in the stocks.

The villagers hailed from different areas around the world, each having their own beliefs about how to kill a vampire. They had been unable to agree on the proper method for disposal of his body, so they decided to prepare for every possible eventuality. He had been killed with a wooden stake, but they finished the job by sawing off his head with a silver dagger. Then his body was burned, and the ashes doused with holy water before being buried in sacred ground.

After Mortecai was dealt with, the villagers returned to the church for one final meeting. They had to decide what to do with the bodies of the murdered villagers. Many of them were related to the three people so emotions ran high. Nobody wanted to disrespect their honored dead, but once again there were disagreements amongst the villagers regarding how one became a vampire.

The raised voices in the church drowned out the noises outside.

O'Malley returned to the village after his first day's slumber in one of the cemetery's crypts as a newly born vampire. He rose to find his feast last night had done little to slacken his hunger... his thirst for the blood of the innocent. He hid his identity under a large woolen cloak, the hood pulled down, obscuring his face. He arrived just in time to see the villagers sever Mortecai's head from his body and then burn his remains.

Relief flooded through him as he realized that the villagers believed themselves free of the demon from Hell.

*My plan worked. Mortecai thought he was so superior to the other villagers. The fool never realized that if he had spoken up immediately, my plan would have been thwarted. In my weakened state during the first hours after my rebirth, they could have prevented me from feeding and building my strength. He was going to die anyway, not last night, but one evening soon... with the rest of them. But now, they believe they have vanquished the vampire, and won't be worried about the real threat... me! It is too late now for them to change their fate.*

But O'Malley was surprised to see the entire village gathering once more in the church.

"What are they up to?" he wondered, and ventured closer to hear what they were saying.

Then he smiled, his fangs sparkling in the moonlight. This was too good to be true. The villagers were scared that one of the three slain townsfolk could rise as a vampire, but they had no idea if that was even possible or how to prevent it. They had already proven that that did not know how to deal with a vampire if they actually found one. From what they were saying, he could tell they had many superstitious beliefs about vampires... beliefs that were entirely false. He'd seen their ignorance on display when they dealt with Mortecai, but this only confirmed it. These fools thought they needed to sever the head, burn the body, or bury the cremains in sacred ground. But none of that did anything. A stake through the heart was all that was needed... a stake carved from an Ebony tree.

They also believed—again, falsely—that vampires could be repelled by holy water or crucifixes, or even garlic! It was all quite ridiculous. Vampires were free to roam around on holy ground without fear of pain or weakness. Even as he listened to them, O'Malley was standing on holy ground himself, right outside the church! He was grateful that he had learned a few more things from his vampire sire that he hadn't passed on to Mortecai.

Suddenly, a plan came to him.

It would provide him with enough nourishment to keep him strong for weeks.

Gleefully, O'Malley retrieved the heavy iron chains that had been used to bind Mortecai and used them to chain the doors to the church. Then he went around the building, closing all the

# Shadow's Gate

storm shutters on the windows, bolting them shut with wooden bars to prevent anyone inside from opening them.

He waited until the townsfolk had finished their meeting, agreeing to sever the heads and burn the three villagers' bodies, and tried to leave before revealing himself. He transformed from his corporeal form into a black mist and drifted in through the crack under the door. But Doc Summers' wife screamed when she saw him as she recognized him as the stranger buried the day before.

"Vampire! Father Donahue, grab the crucifix!" she bellowed as she ran into her husband's arms.

O'Malley rushed the Father, grabbing the crucifix brandished at him and snapping it in half before plunging it into the priest's carotid artery. Bright red blood shot forth from the Father's neck like a fountain. O'Malley stood in front of him, mouth open and head up to catch the fount of blood. The women and children screamed as they streamed past him toward the doors of the church, crashing against them to no avail.

When the stream of blood dried up, O'Malley dropped the Father to the ground in a heap.

He grabbed an old widow and pulled her to him, ripping her throat out with his teeth. The blood spurted onto his face as he buried his mouth in the gaping maw, guzzling the hot, thick blood hungrily. One of the young men tasked with protecting the village charged him as he ate and plunged the other half of the wooden stake from the crucifix into O'Malley's chest. O'Malley's derisive laugh was the last sound the young man heard as his head was ripped from his body with just a small tug from O'Malley's powerful hand.

Six of the forty villagers trapped within the church lay dead by the time O'Malley's thirst was slaked. He wiped his mouth

# Sharon Marie Provost

on the back of his hand—not that it changed much since he was covered in coagulated blood from head to toe—before bidding them goodnight. O'Malley bowed with a flourish as he said, "I think Shakespeare said it best. 'Parting is such a sweet sorrow that I shall say goodnight till it be morrow.' Stay well, my lovelies. I like my blood fresh."

O'Malley left the church and proceeded to the stage office to study the maps. He had days to decide where to move on for his next meal.

# Lost In Time

Lindsay's tires skidded off the pavement as she turned abruptly into the dirt and gravel parking lot at Waffle House. This was exactly what she needed... some serious carb-loading before her great adventure.

Lindsay had always been fascinated with the unexplained, from the paranormal to the unsolved riddles of history. This dream destination offered a little of both.

Lindsay had been a curious girl from the moment she was born—a sense of curiosity only stoked by her father, who liked to explore all that life had in store. She was eager to learn about everything, from how technology and nature worked to the world's unexplained phenomena. Many a weekend was spent with her father traveling to the woods in search of Bigfoot or out into the desert on the hunt for visiting aliens.

# Sharon Marie Provost

Her mom was all in favor of her daughter's intelligent questioning but hoped she would go to college and build a secure future for herself.

Instead, however, Lindsay obtained her degree from the Institute of Metaphysical Humanistic Science, where she studied cryptozoology, ufology, paranormal science, and parapsychology. Her career was focused on paranormal investigations with her local team and media appearances as a paranormal expert. She spent the bulk of her time on her own wildly popular blog, and on work as a social influencer with her Instagram and YouTube pages, which depicted her travels and investigations.

What lay ahead of her today wasn't just any investigation: She was finally going to see the one place she had most wanted to visit since she was a teenager.

When Lindsay walked into the restaurant, the host told her to sit wherever she pleased. In keeping with her loner nature, she chose a seat in the back corner, then looked quickly at the menu. She was less concerned with what was for breakfast than with preparing for the day ahead.

When the waitress came over a few minutes later, Lindsay ordered pancakes, hash browns, eggs, and bacon. Then, as soon as the woman walked away, she pulled out a map and notebook filled with her research about Gold Line Junction.

Five years ago, Lindsay had traveled to one of her other places of interest: Roanoke, North Carolina. It was there, in 1585, that English settlers first attempted to establish a permanent colony in the New World. Sometime in the ensuing five years, before any ship could arrive to visit the colony, all 100-odd colonists disappeared without a trace. By the time a

# Shadow's Gate

new group of settlers arrived, all they found was the Native American word "Croatoan" carved into a tree. It was one of history's greatest mysteries, but the case of Gold Line Junction was even more baffling.

The town had been established in March of 1873 when gold was accidentally discovered there: supposedly after a man's burro escaped its pen one night. When he found it the next morning, it was standing near a rock outcropping that contained a rich vein of gold. So, the legend went, but it was a legend common to more than one Western boomtown, so it was hard for Lindsay to know how much of it was true.

Word of the find spread quickly, and by the summer of 1874, Gold Line Junction had become a bustling town with 254 permanent residents, three saloons, two brothels, two mercantiles, a gold mill, and a variety of other businesses.

It was a typical Western mining town, and it stayed that way until one fateful day, which would become known to all historians familiar with the period as The Vanishing. That day—Wednesday, August 12, 1874—began routinely enough, with the townspeople going about their business as usual. A train had come into town to transport gold to wealthy investors in San Francisco. But the next day, when a stage arrived carrying supplies, there was no trace of the 254 townspeople.

Everything else about the town looked normal, but it appeared as if the people had just vanished in an instant without warning. Food was burned and crusted in the pots on hearths in homes and in the town's lone restaurant. On a table in that same restaurant lay Doc O'Halloran's six-shooter and pack items—which, normally, were never out of his reach. His food also remained on the table, partially eaten. It appeared as if several tables had been occupied by people who had departed suddenly in the middle of their meal.

## Sharon Marie Provost

Wet clothes were found still hanging on a clothesline, with the rest left lying in a laundry basket nearby. The mail was partially sorted on the counter in the Post Office. Oddly though, there was no sign of any emergency that might have prompted the townspeople to leave everything at a moment's notice. No telegraphs had been sent asking for help or giving anyone notice of their departure.

In the years that followed, the site became so famous that preservationists made sure to keep it in good condition. They made sure to keep it just the way it had been found, maintaining and restoring the buildings as needed, and offering tours that regaled visitors with the legend of The Vanishing.

The town was now the focal point of a state park called Gold Line Legacy.

Lindsay was so engrossed in her notes that she wasn't sure how much time had passed since she placed her order. Looking down at her watch to check the time, she noticed the date as well: She was surprised to realize it was August 12$^{th}$. She had been on a road trip visiting old towns in the west for the past few weeks, so it hadn't occurred to her that she was visiting Gold Line Junction on the very date that the townspeople had disappeared.

She was in a hurry to get an early start exploring, so she pointed at her watch when the waitress looked over at her. The waitress finally brought her food a few minutes later, but it seemed like forever to Lindsay.

Lindsay quickly devoured her food and paid her bill as she pondered what she might see at the site. She strode quickly to her Jeep and jumped in, smiling to herself that she was right on

# Shadow's Gate

schedule: With luck, she should arrive just as the state park opened.

A short time later, she pulled up to the gate at the park and dug into her wallet to pull out the money for the entrance fee. The ranger sitting in the small shack at the gate seemed totally engrossed in the book he was reading. He finally looked up when she held the money out over his book.

"Morning," he grumbled.

"Good morning to you. The park seems pretty quiet. Is it usually like this?"

"This park doesn't see much traffic at this time of year... too hot. We close at sundown, so I'll be around to check out the town and shut things down about 8."

"OK. Thanks."

Lindsay took the map of the town he offered her and drove down to the parking area about a mile away. She grabbed her pack with the notebook and stuffed the map inside, along with her water bottle. She'd worn shorts and a tank top, but she was still hot: The temperature was already 85, and it was just 8 a.m. But the heat didn't matter to Lindsay: She was so eager to see the town, she couldn't help but powerwalk down the hill from the parking lot. Based on the pictures she had seen online, she knew the town would be nearly pristine because it had been carefully restored and protected by the Park Service.

The reality didn't disappoint. As Lindsay came around the bend in the trail and caught her first glimpse of Gold Line Junction, she saw that it looked just the way the pictures had shown it... and just as it must have looked on this date in 1874 when everyone disappeared. She slowly strolled through the town, taking in the whole scene and stopping to get some panoramic photos before she began to focus on specific locations.

Pulling out the park map, she plotted out a course to investigate building by building.

Over the years, people familiar with the area had pored over the town, seeking to discover its secret, but no evidence had been found. No one had lived in the area in the years after the disappearance, and most people avoided it altogether, thinking it was cursed. Archaeologists had done a thorough survey but had failed to find an explanation; then the Park Service had looked into the matter, but likewise had come up empty.

Lindsay realized the odds were against her discovering the cause of The Vanishing, but she held out a glimmer of hope that she might succeed where the others had failed. She'd spent years studying mysteries such as these, and she'd solved her fair share of them. This was what she did—what she'd been trained to do.

Lindsay carefully documented her observations about each building, taking photographs from every possible angle. Each of the structures was locked up to preserve the artifacts inside, but she could see through the windows easily.

Staring at the town's reflection in one of those windows, facing the street from one of the two mercantiles, Lindsay became caught up in her thoughts. No matter how many possibilities she considered for the cause of The Vanishing, none of them seemed to make sense. Most frustrating to her was the question of why they would leave no warning, post no notice of explanation, send no telegraphs to family or to those investors in San Francisco.

Lindsay was startled out of her reverie by the sound of a horse whinnying off to her side. As her eyes refocused on the reflection in front of her, she noticed people walking in and out of the saloon behind her. She was sure the doors to the saloon had been bolted shut, just like all the other doors she'd seen in the park. On top of this, the town had been empty when she arrived, and she hadn't noticed anyone else in the streets... until now. And these weren't just any visitors.

It took her a second to process the sight she was beholding. Even odder than seeing people entering a locked building was the way they were dressed: like people straight out of the Old West. She began to wonder just how vivid her imagination could be, and she decided to turn around in an attempt to regain her composure by confronting the reality behind the reflection.

Except what she saw was a bustling Old West town full of horses and settlers, and what she heard was the sound of the mill down the road processing ore: It was nearly deafening.

She turned back around to look at the reflection again, sure that she would see the dead town she had entered. But instead, she saw no reflection at all.

Her head was spinning, and she felt like she was having a panic attack.

She was startled back to her new reality when a booming voice yelled at her, "Tarnation! Get out of the way! Are you daft?" She spun around toward the voice and had to jump out of the way as a heavy wagon came barreling toward her, drawn by two powerfully built horses. She stumbled toward the boardwalk in front of the saloon and sat down heavily.

Her thoughts were a jumble as she tried to make sense of what was happening. It had to be nearly 100 degrees out by now. Could she be suffering from heat stroke? Was she sick? Was she dreaming? She wrenched her water bottle out of her bag and began to down its contents quickly. She scooted back across the boards to get to the shade, desperately thinking that maybe, if she rehydrated herself and cooled down, everything would return to normal.

She closed her eyes and tried to block out the sounds of the town around her.

She didn't know if she fell asleep or passed out, but she awoke with a start when she felt something hard prodding her in the side. The saloon owner stood above her, poking her with a broom.

"No loitering at me bar," he said in a strong Irish accent. "Come in and get a drink, or go sleep off yer drunken stupor elsewhere."

Lindsay slowly stood up and wandered off into the town. She decided to ask some of the people walking past if maybe she was in the middle of some re-enactment or Western Days festival. The ranger hadn't mentioned any events on the schedule today, but then again, she had barely gotten his nose out of that book to take her money. She was looking around, trying to find someone who looked friendly to ask, but they were all giving her hard looks.

Lindsay approached a woman sitting on her porch, singing as she peeled potatoes.

"Excuse me," she said.

The woman looked up at her, curiosity in her eyes.

"I was wondering if you could answer a few questions for me," Lindsay said nervously.

The woman nodded.

"What is the date?"

"Why, it is the 12th of August, 1874. Have you been on a long journey and lost your sense of time?"

# Shadow's Gate

Lindsay stammered, "No. Umm... I mean what date is it really? What event is this? Where did you all come from? I mean... I know you aren't supposed to break character at these things, but I really need to know what's going on."

The woman stared at her, eyes wide.

"Are you all right, miss? I'm not sure what you're talking about. You're in the town of Gold Line Junction. It is August 12, 1874. There is no event going on today that I know of. Just the usual doings in a mining town. Us townsfolk are from all over the place. Some of us traveled across the country for this boom. Others crossed the mountains from San Francisco. We have some immigrants from Ireland, and there are some Chinese that work the mines. Myself, I'm from Virginia City."

"Thank you," Lindsay said as she wandered off, more lost and confused than before. She decided to head back over to the saloon. There seemed to be a lot of people inside. And besides, whose tongue was looser than a drunk lost in their alcohol?

She pushed through the swinging doors and was astounded by the sight before her.

A man was playing a lively tune at the piano as saloon girls wandered around, serving drinks and draping themselves across the patrons. One was up on a small stage at the back, dancing the can-can to the delight of the inebriated men before her. Other men were playing cards and dice games as they drank themselves into a stupor. She wandered over to the bar to speak with the bartender.

"Hello. Are you guys having a Wild West festival here today?" Lindsay asked with a smile.

"No, ma'am. Why do you ask? This is like any other day here in the good ol' Junction."

"What's the date?"

"Hmmm. Let me see," he said as he reached over and grabbed the local newspaper.

"Well, ma'am. It is August 12$^{th}$."

"1874?" she inquired.

"Yes, ma'am."

Lindsay took a seat on the stool before her, utterly confused. She ordered an ale and began to drink it slowly. How could this have happened? At this point, Lindsay was open to any explanation. She believed in the potential existence of ghosts, xenomorphs, creatures such as Sasquatch studied in cryptozoology, and alternate planes of reality. In the little town of Gold Line Junction, could there be a thinning in the boundary that separated these different planes? Could this explain the sudden disappearance of the townspeople? Could she, herself, have gotten caught up in this and lost her own place in time?

Just then, an arm wrapped around her shoulders and pulled her close to the foul-smelling miner next to her.

"Hey there, little lady. Let's go up and have some fun. I just got paid," he purred into her ear.

The foul smell of whiskey on his breath made her gag as she pulled away from him quickly.

"Leave me alone!"

"Whoa there! You're mine now. I have the money to pay your boss for the time. Now come here!" he growled as he yanked her wrist, pulling her back over to him.

Lindsay tried to yank herself free as she continued to protest that she was not for sale. But she was helpless, and the drunkard began to drag her toward the stairs as she cried out in protest. Scanning the room desperately for some means of escape, her gaze fell on a deputy across the bar.

She locked eyes with him and yelled for help.

# Shadow's Gate

The lawman stood up and came over quickly, looking bewildered at the scene before him.

"What's going on here?" he drawled sternly.

Lindsay explained that she was a visitor to Gold Line Junction who'd just come in from out of town. He would have thought her mad if she'd tried to explain the real situation. She told him her assailant seemed to think she was a saloon girl for sale, but that this was simply not the case.

From the look in his eyes, Lindsay could tell she'd gotten through to him. The deputy could see by the way she dressed that she was not a saloon girl and she wasn't from anywhere nearby. In fact, he had never seen anyone dressed quite like her. However, she was clearly distressed and needed help. He removed the miner's hand from her arm and took her other hand to guide her over next to him.

"She's not for sale, Samuel. Leave her be and get back to your drink before I take you in for disorderly conduct to sleep it off."

The deputy turned his back and started to lead Lindsay away from Samuel. She could tell from his expression that he wanted to talk to her: probably to see what business had brought her to the Junction. But her thoughts were interrupted by a gasp from one of the saloon girls, who had seen Samuel reach for his sidearm. Samuel was known to have a temper, and he did not take kindly to someone taking anything or anyone that he felt was rightfully his.

Lindsay and the deputy both turned, just in time to see him fire his weapon.

In nearly the same instant, Lindsay was jarred and felt a searing pain as the bullet entered her chest. She stumbled backward from the force of it, and she fell to the ground, her knees crashing hard into the saloon's wooden floorboard. But she barely noticed as intense pain flooded her upper body. She grew faint as she felt blood pouring from the wound. In desperation, she tried to tell herself that it was all just a dream. The deputy was talking to her, but she couldn't understand him as her eyelids fluttered, and she drifted into unconsciousness.

It was 8:10 in the evening when the park ranger finished his book and set it down. The sun had set a short time before, and twilight was arriving quickly. It was time to make his rounds and close up. As he thought about it, he didn't remember hearing or seeing the woman who'd come in first thing that morning leave the park. She had been the only visitor all day. He climbed into his truck and headed down to the town to remind her it was time to leave.

As he drove by the parking lot, he saw that her Jeep was still there.

He parked at the edge of town and began to look for her. Oddly, she did not appear to be anywhere in sight.

He walked down the boardwalk, first on one side and then the other, calling out for her. As he came to the saloon entrance, he saw a pen on the ground. It caught his attention, but just as quickly, his eyes were drawn to a shocking sight inside the saloon: He was stunned to see the woman's body through the window, lying in a pool of blood in the middle of the barroom.

The ranger grabbed his cell phone and quickly called 911.

He took a step toward the door and tried the handle, only to find it locked. Then he remembered that the keys to all the buildings were kept in the shack back up the road. The rangers rarely entered the buildings, except to clean them every so often, so he wasn't carrying them.

# Shadow's Gate

He ran back to his truck and sped back up the road to grab them. When he returned, he rushed into the building, intent on rendering first aid while he waited for help. But as he reached out and touched the woman, his worst fears were confirmed. She was cold and her body stiff: It was clear that she was beyond medical help.

He backed away quickly and left the building so as not to disturb the scene. Paramedics soon arrived and confirmed that she was deceased. The police were not far behind and began an investigation in earnest. He told them the building had been locked when he arrived. Further investigation found no signs of forced entry. The police then asked him to give them footage from the many security cameras around the park.

The footage at the gate only showed her entering the park. Video taken by perimeter cameras showed no one sneaking into the town from the desert beyond.

Finally, they examined footage from the cameras mounted discreetly throughout the town and inside the buildings. One camera showed her standing outside the mercantile, seemingly staring at something. What it was, they couldn't tell. It was not visible to them. As they watched intently, the video suddenly went dark for one second; the picture returned quickly, but when it did, the woman was no longer there. Another camera inside the saloon had apparently lost signal at the exact same moment. When the picture returned a second later, the woman's body appeared as if by magic inside the saloon, bathed in blood. Investigators had no explanation for the security footage. It showed no signs of being spliced or tampered with, even though what it seemed to show could not possibly have occurred in the brief time the signal was lost.

An autopsy was performed to confirm the cause of death and look for evidence on the body. The manner of death was ruled a homicide. The cause of death was listed as a gunshot wound that penetrated her heart, causing exsanguination. The projectile was sent to ballistics, and the results were puzzling, to say the least: It was found to be a 0.45-caliber bullet from an 1873 Colt Peacemaker Revolver. There were traces of black powder—a substance that had fallen out of use between 1896 and 1905 with the advent of smokeless powder.

To this day, the case remains unsolved.

To this day, the disappearance of the settlers from Gold Line Junction remains unsolved.

Only one person might have been able to explain what happened, but she was murdered on August 12, 2014.

## Shadow's Gate

# Soulmates

**M**eredith questioned whether the experience had even occurred. Shock overtook her mind because she had *seen* him again.

*Was seen even the right word?*

It had been six years since the first time she encountered him on the worst night of her life. Now here she was experiencing another event that had her terrified and wondering if she would survive. And here he was again!

She could still remember that long-ago night, like it had happened yesterday. Right after college, she had moved to San Francisco for an internship that would, hopefully, lead to a long-term position with the firm. With money being short, she lived in a tiny apartment in a low-income neighborhood. One evening, her workday ran quite late. Exhaustion had set in, so her awareness of her surroundings had vanished. She'd never even seen the man coming.

Pain shot through the back of her head, and pinpoints of light flashed in front of her eyes. She stumbled and almost caught herself until a hard shove in the small of her back propelled her onto the ground. She rolled over onto her back, and her world spun. She found it difficult to try to focus in the darkness on the form above her. He dropped to his knees on top of her, pinning her to the ground.

He wrapped his fingers in her hair and bounced her head off the pavement again. Vaguely aware of her surroundings as she fought unconsciousness, she felt him begin to remove her clothes. Her eyelids fluttered, and she struggled to move. As her mind swam ever closer to full awareness, she attempted to call out for help, but only a whisper issued from her lips.

His hand clamped down on her throat, cutting off her air. Her eyes bulged as her face reddened. Her lungs aching for oxygen, she looked up at him, pleading with her eyes for one precious gulp of air.

"Go ahead. I dare you. I WILL hurt you, if you make me. Not one sound... not even a whisper, or I will choke you again. Do you understand?"

His hands gripped her hair again as he growled, "Do not fight me," as he punctuated his threat with her head bouncing off the pavement again. Meredith's eyes closed as she drifted into darkness. She awoke a few minutes later as he violated her body, his grunts of pleasure ringing through her ears. Her mind drifted into the abyss, trying to push away the horror of this moment.

# Shadow's Gate

A shy, quiet girl, Meredith mostly kept to herself. She had never been one to have close friends or attend parties. Even though she was 22, she had never even dated anyone, let alone given herself to a man. The violation of her body was more than her mind could handle, so it drifted into a quiet, dark place... alone.

Except she became aware at some point that she was no longer alone. At first, she could only feel a presence... one that felt soothing and caring. She could feel the sensation of someone softly caressing her forehead and murmuring words of encouragement. She realized that her eyes were staring into the eyes of someone... a man... the kindest, most loving eyes she had ever seen. Almost like the Cheshire Cat, the rest of him wasn't visible—just his eyes—as he tried to comfort her and encourage her to make it through this moment... for him.

*For him? Who the hell was this man? How could some stranger ask her to survive for him?*

And survive is just what Meredith did. She did not fight that violent stranger. When he was done, he left her lying there, battered and broken... emotionally. Meredith, a born fighter, retreated into herself even more, but she poured herself into her work. She worked even longer hours and impressed her employers. Her internship passed in a blur and evolved into her career for the past six years. Her schedule did not leave much time for socializing, but if Meredith was honest with herself, she didn't mind. She could never explain what she had experienced that night, yet somehow, she felt he was somewhere out there waiting for her... as she was waiting for him. As the years passed, her strength in that belief faded, but never disappeared.

Now today, in another time of need, he had appeared again.

# Sharon Marie Provost

A light snow had fallen overnight after rain earlier in the evening, so the roads had become an ice-skating rink. Meredith left early for work to give herself plenty of time for the commute. Unfortunately, others had the same idea... not all of them as careful as Meredith. Meredith approached an intersection and proceeded through as the light turned green. A green Tundra on the cross street approached the intersection— too fast, given the road conditions, to stop before crashing into the driver's side of Meredith's car.

Meredith had seen a flash of movement to her side before she felt the impact. Her whole body was thrown to the side against her safety belt, before her head ricocheted off the driver's window, shattering the already cracked glass. Meredith awoke to splitting pain roaring through her head. Her vision was blurry from the blood streaming into her eyes. Her head throbbed with each strobe of the lights from the emergency vehicles parked around them. She tried to turn her body to unbuckle her seatbelt, but her head began to spin uncontrollably. She heard a faint voice to her side telling her not to move as her world faded to black.

She awoke sometime later strapped to a table, various banging and whirring noises surrounding her... each bang pounding another nail into her brain... or at least that's how it felt. She appeared to be in some kind of tube, but she couldn't focus her thoughts enough to understand her location. A voice drifted down from a speaker above her, telling her to calm down.

"Meredith. Meredith, you are at the hospital. You were in a car accident. We are performing an MRI because you experienced a traumatic brain injury. I need you to hold still for me. Do you understand?"

# Shadow's Gate

Meredith attempted to nod, but her head was strapped down as well. Besides, even the slightest movement sent shock waves of pain through her head. "Yes," she replied in a weak voice as she fought a wave of nausea. She gagged as she struggled to breathe through her nose, fighting the urge to vomit. "I think I am going to throw up!" she blurted mere seconds before another wave fought to overtake her.

"Breathe through your nose, slow and deep. I will be right there. I will pause the scan."

A moment later, the technician whisked into the room, followed by a nurse.

"Her neck was cleared, right?"

"Yes," the nurse replied as she inserted a needle into Meredith's IV line.

"I am giving you Metoclopramide. You should feel better soon. Just try to relax and keep breathing through your nose."

The technician ripped open the Velcro strap securing Meredith's head. She slid one arm under her upper back, as she stated, "I will help you sit up... slowly. There is a basin on your right side if you need to vomit."

As she sat up, the dizziness and nausea increased. She reached out for the basin as she began, "Thank y.... huuuuuuuurrrggggghh!" Her head whipped down into the basin, as she began to vomit repeatedly. Her vision began to fade once more to black as she finally lifted her head. The technician, at the ready, caught her and laid her back down on the table to finish the scan. She called out into the hall to catch the nurse's attention so she could check her vitals.

Meredith once again awoke to a whirring sound, but this one came from right atop her head. She was in pre-op, getting her head shaved as they prepared her for an emergency craniotomy. The surgical technician noticed her regain consciousness.

"Meredith, can you hear me?"

"Yes," she whispered.

"You have a bleed in your brain, which is causing a dangerous increase in intracranial pressure... it is pushing on your brain. We are taking you into emergency surgery shortly. Please stay calm. You will be ok."

Meredith began to panic—her thoughts all mixing together—as she began to contemplate what could happen.

*I am not ready to die. I am too young. But what if they save me, only for me to be a vegetable? My intelligence is my best attribute. I need my brain. I haven't found him yet. It is not my time.*

Her breathing quickened and her pulse raced as she began to worry if she would ever meet him... her soulmate. She started to feel lightheaded again as her vision began to blur. Then a calm draped her, as she saw those eyes, *his eyes*, once more. Just as before, she felt him softly rubbing her forehead as he whispered his love to her.

"Calm down, babe. Everything is going to be okay. I am here with you, now and for always. You need to relax, so they can take care of you. I can't lose you. You are my angel. You are my world. I can't go on without you. I love you more."

The surgical technicians rushed her into the OR as her blood pressure began to plummet. Her head lolled to the side as she murmured, "No, I love you more."

Twenty-four hours later, Meredith began to stir. A nurse was checking her vitals at the time, so she called the doctor to let him know she had regained consciousness. As her eyelids struggled to open, she heard the nurse say, "You scared us there. We nearly lost you, but you are a fighter. How are you feeling?"

# Shadow's Gate

Her mouth felt full of cotton, but she managed to reply, "Pain."

"Your head?"

Meredith held up her thumb in the affirmative.

"Do you think you can swallow a pill?"

"Yes."

"I will go get you some Tylenol. We can't give you any opiates right now because we need to be able to assess any change in your mental status properly."

Meredith spent the days and weeks that followed recovering from the brain injury and its myriad side effects, spending countless hours in occupational and physical therapy. By afternoon each day, her mind and body were spent, but she couldn't help but lie in bed wondering if her vision of him was real now... or ever had been. As intelligent as Meredith might be, that intelligence did not preclude her from beliefs in the possibility of the paranormal or other preternatural occurrences.

It wasn't just the words he said or the way he looked at her—the overwhelming feeling of calm that enveloped her... the recognition she felt both for him and from him. Not just familiarity, but the way she felt in love with him, had always loved him for all time; that was why she couldn't get him out of her mind. Yet, her logical mind, ever-present, reminded her that she had not met him in the past six years. What was she... or he... waiting for? If they were meant to be together, why hadn't they found each other yet? More importantly, if he was her soulmate, why did he only appear when she faced great peril, almost as if he were just a coping mechanism conjured up by a desperate brain facing the possibility of death?

Finally, the day came for Meredith's release from the hospital. Weeks of recovery still lay ahead before she could return to work or any semblance of her normal life. She was troubled by temporary lapses in short term memory, and the doctor said that could continue for the next several months. Plus she faced a rigorous schedule of rehabilitation and physical therapy, but at least she could get some real sleep in her own bed. The hospital had set her up with a service that would transport her to her appointments until she was cleared to drive again.

To her dismay, Meredith realized no matter how much of a loner she might be, she did miss having the hustle and bustle of people around her and occasionally interacting with her, whether it be at work or more recently at the hospital. She had plenty to keep her busy with the homework she was given after her therapy sessions, but she needed something more.

Perish the thought, but she found herself joining a singles chat room. Typical of Meredith, she did her research and found one with a variety of rooms that focused on topics ranging from sports to movies and even politics, as well as the expected ones geared towards finding a mate. She entered the room simply titled "Chit-Chat," surprised to find a lively discussion about her guilty pleasure, the TV show *Married at First Sight*.

This season was a delight to the viewer who loves dumpster fires, but an absolute travesty when one considered the poor, incompatible couples paired up by the so-called experts. One had to question what they were thinking when one of the marriages never even happened; the bride bailed out on the first episode without even saying "I do." Meredith felt terrible that she was finding such enjoyment at the expense of others, yet she couldn't help but feel better when she found a whole group of people doing the same. Meredith's spirits rose over the next two weeks, as she spent her downtime online chatting about various topics with her new "friends."

Meredith went to the kitchen to make herself a cup of green tea. As she waited for the kettle to heat up, she heard an unfamiliar bong sound on the computer. She was accustomed to the tiny ding as new messages appeared in the chat screen, but this was different. She limped over to check and found a "1" appearing over the envelope at the top that indicated she'd received a private message. While she thought of these people as her so-called friends, she didn't intend to a real relationship with any of them. They were simply a distraction... a way to keep her mind busy without overwhelming her.

She had joined a singles chat room after all, so she was afraid of what she might find if she opened that private message.

*A nude pic of some rando guy, or God forbid, a dick pic... now that is the last thing I want to see at this moment.*

But, to her surprise, she felt drawn, no, compelled, to open the message. Her gaze was only drawn away from the screen when the teapot began to whistle. She tore herself away from the computer long enough to pour the water into her waiting cup and move the kettle off the heat. Now that she had walked away, she had a moment to ponder whether to open that message.

*What would I gain from opening it? I am certainly not looking for a real friendship with these people, yet alone a romantic one. But... is there any harm in just looking?*

Meredith strolled back over to the computer and clicked on the envelope as she sat down. She couldn't help but giggle when the message came up from someone with the screen name "Passion8one." But upon reading it, she was shocked to find a very sweet, intelligent note.

"Hello, Scarletnerd. Your screen name intrigued me. Why

Scarletnerd? I have seen some of your interactions with other users in the group. I find you truly fascinating, humorous, and full of astute observations. I was hoping that maybe we could chat one day."

Meredith was surprised to find her fingers on the keyboard tapping out a quick response. She felt a *need* to talk to him.

"Hi, Passion8one. I have to ask because your screen name is very interesting as well. What are you passionate about? To be totally honest, I didn't notice you in the chat room, but then again, I haven't taken notice of any person in that group. I am just there to fill time and for a little human interaction while I'm stuck at home recovering."

Meredith pressed "send" before she could reconsider, but gasped when she saw the message was opened immediately. She hadn't checked to see if the sender was online right now.

*Too late now!*

She chewed on her lower lip with anxious anticipation.

*He probably won't answer now. Good job, Meredith! Smooth move, Ex-Lax! Tell him you haven't noticed him, because you don't care about ANYBODY in the group. What is with your overblown need to be honest? Whoa, whoa, whoa! Why do I care so much if he answers?*

As she stared off into space arguing with herself, she jumped when she heard another bong as a new private message appeared. He had answered!

"LOL. Nice to meet you officially, Scarletnerd. To answer your question, I am passionate about my work... and those I care about. You said you are home recovering. I hope you are doing well."

"I must be brain damaged. *giggling* Pardon my dark humor. I didn't mean to sound so dismissive and uninterested earlier. I am just an introvert by nature. As for how I am doing, I

# Shadow's Gate

have a long road ahead of me, but I am improving each day. I was in a bad car accident and sustained a severe head injury. They had to do emergency surgery to relieve the pressure on my brain, plus repair some fractures. I haven't been cleared to drive yet, so I am stuck at the house, except for my therapy and doctor appointments."

"Wow. I am so sorry to hear that. I completely understand... I took no offense. I am an introvert myself. I wouldn't normally just contact someone like this, but I rarely find someone as intelligent as you. It is even rarer to find someone who thinks like I do."

"Oh great, I am so happy I didn't offend you. And sorry for the long diatribe about my injury. You certainly didn't ask to know all that. What did you mean about 'someone who thinks like you?"

"Well, I saw some of your comments regarding *Married at First Sight*. Most people disagreed with you, but you stood firm, and I totally agree with your observations about the couples. You seem to have similar political views as well. I just thought we could get along well and enjoy good conversation. So, tell me more about yourself... your career... Do you have pets? Favorite books? Are you married?"

"LMAO. Well, clearly, I do like my reality TV, at least right now when all I have is time. I work at an engineering firm. I don't have any pets right now, but I am considering getting a dog. I could use a little company on the long, cold evenings. I am an avid reader and horror movie fan... Stephen King, Dean Koontz, Clive Barker. But I do love true crime, the classics, Nicholas Sparks... well pretty much all books really. And finally, no, I am not married. By the way, my name is Meredith. Same questions to you."

"Oh yes, I suppose introductions should have been first. My name is Gabriel. I am an analyst, so I can work from home whatever hours I choose. I have one cat named Alex. He is an extremely independent cuss and not much company at all. LOL. I am not much of a reader myself. I don't normally watch a lot of TV either, but I somehow got interested in *Married at First Sight*. I was married many years ago when I was young, but it didn't work out."

The next three hours passed without either of them knowing how long they had been chatting online. It was only when the doorbell rang that Meredith realized the time. Her ride was here to take her to physical therapy. She excused herself, thanking him for the pleasant afternoon spent chatting. She told the driver she would be right out and then hurried back to the computer. Meredith then did something she would have never expected she would do. She clicked on the attachment link in the chat window and sent him a picture of herself. She quickly followed that up with a message, "Can you please send me a picture of you? I want to know what my new friend looks like." Then she logged off before he could answer.

Meredith found herself distracted and unable to follow the therapist's directions. She couldn't get the conversation with Gabriel out of her mind. She had never connected with someone so fast before. It was like they were two halves of the same whole. They had so many things in common, and it wasn't like either one of them was just agreeing with the other. They both could go on at length about whatever the subject may be. Passionate was definitely the proper adjective to describe him.

But she wasn't just puzzled by their similarities—it was more than that. It was the sense that she knew him somehow, like she had known him her whole life. She told him things

# Shadow's Gate

about her life that she had never told anyone else. She couldn't remember how the subject even came up, but she told him about her attack in college. He had been shocked, but pleasantly surprised, by her honesty with him in their first conversation. He had even apologized; in case he had caused her to mention a topic that brought up such bad memories.

She felt irresistibly drawn to him. She wanted... needed... him in her life, like they were meant to be together forever.

*I am losing my mind. Maybe I should talk to my neurologist. Maybe this is one of those changes in behavior that they need to monitor. Two months ago, I wasn't even looking for a relationship. Someday, eventually, a husband and a family would be nice. But not right now, not while I am actively pursuing my career. There is simply no time for that. Or is it exactly the right time? If anything, adulthood has shown me that life is too short. One never knows when her time might be up. I have always dreamed about finding my Prince Charming... my soulmate... since I was a little girl in pigtails. Maybe I should see where this goes. There is just something about him.*

Meredith returned home from her appointment and spent the evening relaxing in front of the television. The next morning, she awoke dreaming about a life with Gabriel. She didn't even know what he looked like, so the entire time she saw him from a profile angle or from behind. Just before she woke, he turned to face her, and all she saw was those eyes. The eyes that had haunted her for the last six years. The eyes of her protector. The eyes of the man she loved. Every nerve in her body felt electric. She was simultaneously thrilled and unnerved. She couldn't understand why she would see that in her dream in connection with a man she had just met.

She began her day with her home physical therapy exercises to expend the nervous energy she felt inside. Then she sat down to read the back issues of the quarterly *Engineering Digest*. She couldn't bring herself to log back onto her computer. She needed more time to think rationally. Before she knew it, the entire afternoon had passed. She finally convinced herself to log in just after dinner as she turned on her favorite show. Surely, he would be on so they could discuss Tammy and Ian's disastrous relationship.

She logged on to find he had answered her question from the previous day with a short message, "Hi, babe. I am nothing special. I don't feel comfortable sending a picture of me. I am really not very good looking." However, he never showed up online that night. In fact, he wasn't on the next day or for the next several days after that. She began to fear the worst, thinking she had scared him off by being too forward or too honest. It must be her fault, after all; he was nearly perfect, whether he was handsome or not. She cared more about the man inside than his physical features.

Then five days after they met, she logged onto her chat room and once again found that amazing "1" glowing above the envelope icon. Initially, she feared that her hopes were getting the best of her. Maybe somebody else had messaged her. Maybe he'd finally gotten up the courage to say "Sorry, I am not interested." Then she noticed she also had a new notification. The notification stated that Passion8one had accepted her friend request. Her cursor flew across to the envelope to see his message.

"Hello, Meredith. I am sorry I have not been on the past few days. You mean a lot to me. I just wanted to let you know that I really enjoyed the other day. We have much to discuss. I will talk to you tomorrow, I hope."

Her eyes drifted to the time and date stamp.

# Shadow's Gate

*Yes! He sent that at 11:03. last night. That means he will be on sometime today.*

Almost as if by magic, that bong sound announced the arrival of a new message.

"I thought I might find you on. How are you today, Meredith?"

A wide grin spread across her face as she began to type, "I am doing wonderful. How about you?"

"I am doing well. I missed you. I mean, I missed talking to you. I really enjoyed our previous conversation. How has your week been?"

"My week has been fabulous. I have made great strides the past few days in my physical therapy. I may be released to normal activity—and, better yet, driving—as soon as a month from now. I missed you, too. I thought maybe you had lost interest... in our friendship I mean... when I didn't hear from you. How was your week?"

"I had a very busy work week, plus some appointments. I am sorry I didn't get back to you."

"No problem. That is totally fine. I am just glad that everything is okay."

"Well, to be honest, I was a little startled by the strength of our connection. I needed a few days to think. To see how I felt. And I found I wanted to talk to you again. You are an angel, and I couldn't wait any longer."

"I felt, or should I say feel, the same way. I was very happy to see your message when I logged on."

Meredith and Gabriel once again talked for hours, seemingly in the blink of an eye. The conversations were natural and flowed from one topic to the next: his favorite artist, their past relationships (or lack thereof for Meredith), their childhood, favorite movies, music. They simultaneously got to know each other as each affirmed the fact in their own minds that they already did know each other. Gabriel took a deep breath and seemed reluctant to say his next thought. Meredith waited for him to continue; the silence between them did not feel awkward.

"I am drawn to darkness. Do you know what I mean?"

"Yes, I think I do. I love the dark and twisty side of life. You probably noticed that with my joke that first day about being brain damaged. If you don't laugh, you will cry. And who wants that? I especially love extreme horror movies like those from the French. Vampires are my absolute favorite. I have been drawn to them since I was a little girl."

Meredith's voice dropped to a whisper, "I feel like I am a vampire. Or at least, I wish I was one."

"I knew it. I, too, am drawn to vampires. You do understand, I think. But vampires are not just blood-thirsty monsters as the mainstream media has depicted them. There are other kinds. Some feast off the energy of others, not just any person, not without permission, and not in a harmful way. They feed in a mutual exchange of energy, giving their own soul and energy as they take in their partner's—the two souls intertwining as they meet and pass between them. And it only works with their true partner... their soulmate. I hope you know what I mean. I hope you don't think I am weird."

Meredith's brow furrowed as she pondered the meaning of his words. Or more to the point, her feelings about them. She did know what he meant. Thinking about that exchange of energy made her feel warm and excited... hungry even. She may not have thought about it in exactly those terms, but that had always been part of her vision of her soulmate. Only one person

# Shadow's Gate

in the world could be right for her. Only one person could feed her soul and make her happy. They each would feed off the other's joy and energy, fulfilling each other in a way no one or nothing else could.

Her voice was serious but excited as she murmured, "Yes. I know exactly what you mean."

"I thought you might. I am glad you understand."

"I do. Are you saying what I think you are saying?"

His voice wavering and unsteady, Gabriel replied, "Yes. That is how I feel. I have always felt that way. I believe I am one of those energy vampires. I have been with other partners, but no one else was ever right. No one else was ever like me. I couldn't feed on them. It wouldn't have worked. They were not the same as me, but I think you are."

"Yes. Yes, I am. I have never let myself consciously accept this side of me. But this is how I have always felt. I never dated anyone because I always knew they weren't the same. I have been waiting my whole life to find someone like me. This may sound crazy. I hope you will keep talking to me after this. I feel like I have always known you. I think we are soulmates, fated to be together through all time, living different lifetimes as different people but always together. Ummm..."

"I don't think you are crazy. I feel the same connection with you. It is like we have been together a long time, even though we just met. Were you going to say something else? I felt like you hesitated there."

"Before I tell you, will you humor me? Can you send me a picture of yourself? It really is important to me and to what I tell you."

The pause was interminable, but a response finally arrived.

"Okay. I am still hesitant, but if we are soulmates, then I suppose you should know what I look like."

# Sharon Marie Provost

A moment later, Meredith downloaded the attachment that popped up. Her heart jumped at the sight. First of all, no matter what he said, he was a handsome man. However, it was the eyes that held her attention—the same eyes that had captured her heart all those years ago. Just as she had suspected after her dream, somehow this man was the one who had come to her in her times of need. It took her a few moments to deal with the shock. She couldn't decide whether she should tell him or not. The whole idea was preposterous, yet... true. She didn't realize how long she had left him hanging until the sound announced another message.

"I guess you don't like my picture. I was afraid of that. I am sorry to have bothered you."

"No, no, wait please!"

"Yes?"

"This is really hard for me to say. This sounds absolutely crazy, and I am terrified I will scare you away if I tell you. But I can't hold it back any longer. I feel like you have been coming to me, in times of need, for the past six years. I think we felt each other out there, so there was like a psychic connection, at least emotionally."

"I don't understand. What do you mean?"

"I told you how I was attacked six years ago. While I was lying there, dying inside, I saw a pair of eyes, *your eyes*, in my mind. Those eyes looked at me with more love than I can possibly express. They showed the pain that they felt, you felt, seeing me lying there in such pain. I heard a soothing voice murmuring words to calm me. I felt like that presence was softly rubbing my head to help me cope. Then again, a few months ago when I had my car accident, I saw those same eyes when I started to decompensate in the OR. You told me that you couldn't lose me, and you would be with me forever. You said I was your angel. I didn't mean to leave you hanging after you sent me your picture. I was just so happy to see that it was you. By the way, you lied to me."

"Lied?"

"You are an extremely handsome man. I would feel honored to be seen by your side."

"You are making me blush. You are the gorgeous one."

"So…"

"I don't quite know what to say. It is hard for me to understand. Yet, I believe you. When you told me about your attack, it was very hard for me to listen to because I felt your pain. I could almost see in my mind what had happened to you. I didn't say too much at the time because I couldn't process it all. And as I said, I certainly feel this timeless connection with you."

"This is a 'Meredith telling you everything about herself' day. I didn't get back online that night we first talked because I was terrified of what I was feeling… and thinking. Part of me, although I didn't admit it at first, felt this connection halfway through our first talk. By the end, I felt that I loved you and that we would be together forever. I know that sounds nuts, but it is true."

"I love you, too."

"I love you more."

"More than I love you?"

"No. Some time ago I saw this wall hanging with a quote on it, and it resonated with me in a way I couldn't explain. I knew that is how I would feel when I found my person. *You.*

It said,

## Sharon Marie Provost

"When I say I love you more,
I don't mean I love you more
than you love me. I mean
I love you more than the bad
days ahead of us. I love you
more than any fight we will
ever have. I love you more than
the distance between us. I love
you more than any obstacle that
could come between us."

"That is beautiful. I feel the same way."

"Now that we have said it, I can't say it enough. I love you. I need to see you. LOL. This is going to sound funny, but where do you live? We never covered that. We have discussed most of our lives, yet somehow never where we live. I am in the Bay Area of California."

"I live in Central Oregon. A long distance away, but far from impossible. How about we meet in Mt. Shasta? It's about the halfway point between us. We can see how we connect in person and figure out what to do from there."

"That is perfect. It will be a couple more weeks or so before I can drive, but we will plan something as soon as possible."

Gabriel did not have to work the next day, so they continued their conversation. Before they knew it, the birds were chirping with the sunrise the following day. The ensuing weeks were spent texting each other throughout the day. Since Gabriel worked remotely, he was free to chat back and forth while he worked. Meredith went to her doctor's appointments brighter and happier than the medical staff had ever seen her, and they noticed her recovery had sped up as well. She

# Shadow's Gate

approached her therapy with renewed vigor; she had been no slouch to begin with, but now she exceeded even the therapist's highest expectations. Meredith spent her evenings on the phone, engrossed in conversation with Gabriel.

Two weeks after their enlightening conversation, Meredith had another doctor's appointment to assess her recovery. The visit went better than she could have imagined. The doctor said she might still have periodic issues with her memory, so it was important that she keep her stress level low. However, he had released her to drive again. Even better, he said she could start working a few hours a week at home for the next few weeks. Then she could return to work part-time for a couple of weeks. If all went well, she would be allowed to return full-time after that.

She had planned to have the driver take her to the grocery store after her appointment, but she had him take her home instead. She texted Gabriel on the way to see if he could take a call from her in a few moments, and he said he could. She ran... literally ran... to the couch and began punching the buttons to call him. In a breathless rush, she asked, "When can you take off a few days? How about the 20th?"

"What? What do you mean? Are you okay? Is something wrong?"

"I was released today, just now. I am free! I can drive! I want to see you. I *need* to see you and hold you. I love you so much, sweetheart."

"Oh my god, I am so happy for you. For us. Give me just a few minutes. I will call you back," he said and then hung up.

Meredith laughed as she set the phone down on the coffee table, then proceeded to her computer. She emailed her boss letting him know what the doctor had ordered. Her boss emailed back a few minutes later and suggested she come by the office the next day to discuss a project to work on at home for the next few weeks. He said he would expect her back at work part-time at the start of the month, giving her three weeks to meet with Gabriel when he was available.

Just as she turned away from the computer, the phone rang. Gabriel's excited voice greeted her, "Hey, babe. How about we meet on the 21st at the Shasta Inn? I booked a two-queen-bed cabin with a fireplace. I hope that wasn't too presumptuous. Plus, the inn also has its own restaurant and a bar, so we can spend lots of time together without making you do too much walking."

"That sounds absolutely perfect. Thank you, sweetheart. How many days can you stay? I can't wait to see you! I can't believe that it is only four days away. I am assuming check-in is at 3 p.m.?"

"I have one week off, and I am spending it all with you... every possible moment, even if I have to drive home all night and go to work the next day. You are correct about the check-in time, so I thought we could meet at 5 p.m. at the restaurant. That should give you plenty of time to drive up, including breaks. Are you sure you are up for such a long drive?"

"Of course, I am. Wild horses couldn't stop me. I have to go figure out what to pack. I want to look my best for you. We'll talk later?"

Gabriel's booming laugh filled her ears before he said, "Of course. You are my beautiful, gal. You would look beautiful in a burlap sack. But it might be kind of itchy."

Meredith spent the rest of the afternoon pulling clothes out of her closet, until she finally settled on just the right look. Then she started dinner and texted Gabriel as she cooked. He was

# Shadow's Gate

busy working to wrap up a project before his vacation, so she said goodnight. She could barely sleep that night as her mind was filled with visions of how their first meeting would go.

She rose the next day bright and early, exhausted but happy. She checked her phone and found a message from Gabriel apologizing for being busy the night before. She told him not to worry and then prepared to go meet her boss. She couldn't help but feel excited and a little nervous about driving again for the first time since the accident. However, the drive went fine, as did the meeting. Better than fine, in fact, so she trotted to the car to call Gabriel. The preparation for the project was really just research before she was given the lead in designing a new earthquake-safe arch bridge. She was excited that her boss trusted her to lead such an important project, especially after her injury.

"Congratulations, babe! I am not surprised. Now, we must celebrate, too. Champagne and dinner... the works!"

The next few days passed quickly, as they both immersed themselves in work, then spent all their free time chatting on the phone or texting. Meredith's stress level was a little high, triggered by her determination to succeed on her first big project and the anxiety and anticipation of her meeting with Gabriel. She became so engrossed in the bridge research that she didn't head to bed until 2 a.m. the night before her trip.

The next day, Meredith rose early to start the drive.

A drive to where though?

She had always considered herself late if she arrived on time, so she knew she needed to get going.

She had this overwhelming belief that she needed to be at the Shasta Inn in Mt. Shasta at 5 p.m. to do something or meet someone, but she could not remember what. And the more she focused on that mystery, the more unsure she felt. As she wracked her brain, trying to remember, she began to develop a migraine headache—the kind she had been prone to ever since the accident.

The doctor had told her to remain calm in situations like this because the memory loss was temporary. The best she could do was follow her instincts, calm down, and hope it would all work out if she did.

She arrived in Mt. Shasta around noon and stopped to get some lunch at a delightful outdoor cafe. She read a book and sipped on Diet Coke for the next several hours as she waited for her memory to return.

But still, she couldn't remember why she was there.

She took a short walk on a local nature trail to stretch her legs; then, at 3 p.m., she decided to go check out the inn. She stopped at the lobby desk to see if anyone had been asking for her, but the attendant hadn't seen anyone.

More confused than ever, she walked across the parking lot to the umbrella-covered tables on the lawn. She dearly hoped that either someone would recognize her sitting there or her memory would return by 5 o'clock. She returned to reading her book while she waited.

To her dismay, 5 p.m. came and went without an answer coming to her. A few people arrived for dinner at the restaurant, but they didn't appear to be looking for anyone. She kept waiting, hoping, but at 7:12 p.m., she finally decided it was hopeless.

Discouraged, she made up her mind to drive back toward home and stop for a room somewhere when she got tired. Then she planned to schedule an appointment with her doctor the next day to discuss what had happened. She still couldn't figure out if she had imagined having planned this trip or what she

# Shadow's Gate

might have forgotten.

As she started back across the lot to her car, out of the corner of her eye, she saw a man getting out of his car in the distance. Not wanting to interact with anybody, she kept her head down as she walked, but then she heard her name. She looked up in surprise to see who had called her. He walked forward a few feet as she stopped and stared at him. His face registered relief and happiness at seeing her... but why?

She couldn't stop staring into his eyes as she asked, "Do I know you?"

"Yes, angel. Come here."

He could see the fear and confusion in her eyes, so he held his arms out to her. Without even realizing it, she walked toward him, drawn into his embrace. He wrapped his arms around her gently and held her close, bending down to kiss her forehead as he murmured, "Hi. angel." His soft kisses trailed down her face until he reached her lips. Both of them jumped as they felt the electricity pass between them.

She looked up into those eyes and melted into his arms crying, as she whispered, "Gabriel?"

"Yes, babe."

Recognition dawned on her face, and she launched herself into his arms. She smiled and stood up on her tiptoes to meet his lips. All sense of time and location was lost to them as they were locked in their embrace, feeding from each other. Just as they had discussed, Meredith felt their energies swirling and mixing together and then passing back and forth between them. She had never felt complete before, but now she had found her other half. The sound of a car finally brought Meredith around, as she realized they were in the middle of the road. They moved over against his car, staring at each other, still stunned that they were finally together. She was his, and there was no denying it.

"You looked so upset and confused. Where were you going?" Gabriel queried.

Meredith gave a wry laugh as the tears continued down her face before she answered, "See! I told you I was brain damaged. You deserve someone whole and unbroken. What if this memory loss keeps happening? I couldn't remember who I was coming to see or what I was going to do. I just knew I had to be here at 5 p.m. It was 5, right? Why weren't you here? I nearly left."

"Shhh, shhh, baby. Everything is going to be okay, my angel. I am so sorry I wasn't here on time, sweetheart! My car broke down, and I couldn't get any cell reception. I got here as fast as I could. I don't know what I would have done if I had missed you. But now we have our whole lives together. I know you feel it, too. We may only be together for the next week... right now. But that is not the end for us; instead, it is only the beginning. Am I right?"

"Yes! Yes, it is only the beginning. I am so happy you said that. I feel the same. Now what are we going to do?"

Gabriel wrapped his arm around her—his hand settling on the small of her back. They began walking toward the lobby to check into their cabin. "Now, we go plan our life together. I remember you said you always wanted a fall wedding. Are you busy this September?"

# Shadow's Gate

# Thanksgiving

Thanksgiving morning dawned crisp and clear. Bethany could barely contain her excitement. She rose with the sun and dressed hurriedly so she could go down to the kitchen to help her mother prepare the feast. Thanksgiving had always been her favorite holiday, and it was even more important than usual because they had so much to be thankful for this year. Plus, Daddy had procured some extra-special delicacies for dinner.

She was delighted when her parents allowed her to invite her new friend over for dinner. Bethany had befriended Alice, a local orphan, from the orphanage down the road. Alice had been abandoned outside the local hospital when she was only a few days old, so she had never savored a delicious, extravagant holiday meal with all the fixings.

The home was short-staffed, and its funding was nearly non-existent. The case workers had very little time—and even less compassion—so they didn't really care where Alice went or for how long. It would be one less burden that day to keep them away from celebrating with their own families.

Bethany was determined that she would give Alice the experience of a lifetime.

Bethany's mother, Sophia, was just finishing filling the pièce de résistance with sausage stuffing. Bethany ran over to grab the butter and began slathering the skin liberally. Then she sprinkled parsley over the top before returning it to the refrigerator to await further preparation later.

"What's next, Momma? The berry compote or the pudding?"

"Let's prepare the pudding so it can set up properly before dessert tonight."

Bethany dutifully gathered the ingredients from the pantry and refrigerator for her as her mother grabbed mixing bowls and measuring spoons. The smell of the pudding was strong and so enticing as they mixed it up. Bethany's stomach began to growl angrily. She ran into the pantry and grabbed some cracklins out of the jar to soothe her empty belly. Her mother always had some prepared for just such an occasion. When she returned, the pudding was beautifully smooth and a gorgeous dark reddish-brown color, so she took it from her mother and placed it in the refrigerator.

The morning passed in a whirlwind of activity as her sisters joined the fray in the kitchen, along with her aunts, who had just arrived from out of town. She fought the urge to dip her finger into the tempting berry compote filled with glistening blood red berries. Her nose was filled with the tangy aroma, but she forced herself to place it in the refrigerator untouched.

They seasoned the butt roast and prepared the red glaze to apply at the last minute. Finally, it was time to prepare the sides, including green beans with crushed cracklins on top, mashed potatoes made with fresh milk and butter, and the beet salad and tomato soup appetizers. The flavors and colors of the food perfectly reflected the tastes, smells, and hues of the end of the harvest and beginning of the holiday season. Bethany couldn't have been prouder of the gourmet meal they had painstakingly prepared.

She helped her mother clear and clean the countertops and took out the trash. She piled all the dishes into the sink, and then turned eagerly to her mother, pleading with her eyes.

"Off, you! Thank you for all your help. Go clean up and get ready for your friend's arrival."

Bethany stripped off her apron with a squeal and rushed out of the room. Sophia laughed merrily as she began scrubbing the dishes. A small frown creased her brow as she dearly hoped that Thanksgiving would live up to her daughter's expectations. Bethany had been such a sweet but lonely girl until she met Alice. But their lives are so very different... their upbringing and values so disparate, that she worried that this meal would not go as planned. Bethany would be heartbroken if her friend was uncomfortable or did not enjoy the intricate delicacies they had prepared. This day could go tragically wrong.

*Stop this. This is silly. Everything will be fine.* Sophia shook her head and redoubled her efforts, cleaning the dishes. Much remained to be done still before the rest of the guests arrived, so she had no time to focus on paranoia.

# Sharon Marie Provost

*The world is a different place now. There is plenty of room for different cultures and traditions. Dear Alice is used to peanut butter and jelly as her daily meal. Surely, she will appreciate all the effort we have put into today. Her wee belly will never have been so full and satisfied.*

Bethany washed up and put on her best dress. She laid out all her favorite toys on her bed, and at her tiny table with the tea party already arranged. She even got out a few of her favorite books and put them in the window nook. She wanted Alice to have her choice of activities, so she would have the time of her life and want to visit often. Finally, it was nearly time, so she ran downstairs and out onto the sidewalk.

She looked up the block and saw Alice exit the home. Bethany skipped up the road and met her halfway. The girls greeted each other happily, with hugs and kisses.

"Oh, Bethany! You look so pretty. That dress is amazing," Alice said dejectedly, as she looked down at her own threadbare romper dress and turtleneck shirt.

"Surprise! Guess what?"

"What?" Alice asked shyly.

"I have a matching dress waiting for you in my room. Let's go!"

The girls tore off down the street, giggling the whole way. They entered the house with a clatter and ran up the stairs. Alice began to cry when she entered the room and saw the dress waiting for her. "Are you sure?"

"Yes, silly. You put on the dress, and I will get us a snack before dinner while you change. Be right back."

Alice went to the bathroom to wash up and comb her hair before donning the pristine dress. She had never worn something so fancy before... or new, so she didn't want to dirty it. Bethany reappeared with a chocolate bar for Alice and some

# Shadow's Gate

more cracklins for herself. She knew Alice loved chocolate, so she had gone to the market the day before to buy her one. They ate their snacks, then spent the rest of the afternoon playing. The house was filled with the sounds of the girls' laughter and the conversations of the adults; the volume rising steadily as the number of guests increased throughout the day.

"Bethany! Alice! It's time to wash up for dinner"

The girls jumped up excitedly, nearly knocking each other over as they rushed to the bathroom door simultaneously. They thundered down the stairs, and then forced themselves to enter the dining room calmly.

Alice was overwhelmed by the sheer volume of food she found piled on the table. The aromas were pungent, yet somehow interesting. Alice couldn't even identify the vast majority of the dishes.

Albert, Bethany's father, said a small thanks for all the blessings of the past year. Then the family began to serve themselves family style, passing each of the dishes around the table one-by-one. Sophia piled her plate high, then asked Albert and one of her sisters for help bringing in the two entrées.

Alice's mouth watered at the thought of meat... real meat. The best she could hope for at the orphanage occasionally was canned meat, such as tuna, Vienna sausages, or Spam. The girls dove into their plates as they waited for the adults to return. Alice couldn't resist the berry compote, so she dipped a finger into the bowl and sucked it off greedily. Her face scrunched up at the unfamiliar, metallic taste.

"What is this?" she mewled unhappily.

"Blood compote! You know the popping boba balls people get in tea and on frozen yogurt? I thought it would be fun to have popping boba blood balls in the compote. You know how much I like science. It's really cool molecular gastronomy to make these. Do you like them?" Bethany said in a breathless rush.

"Ewwww! Oh my god! Actual blood? From what? From who? Are you just teas… " Alice's voice trailed off in a breathless whisper as her eyes grew wide. She began to hyperventilate as she watched Albert, Sophia and Sophia's sister bring in the main dishes. In the middle of the table, right in front of Alice, Albert placed an enormous platter with a body on it trussed up like a turkey. But it wasn't a turkey. It was the body of a man; not just any man, but grumpy old Mr. McAllister. His belly was slit wide open, and blood was oozing out of the cavity that was filled with stuffing.

"I want the drumstick," Bethany's sister cried out as she reached forward and began sawing off one of his legs.

Bethany reached forward and began scooping out some stuffing, offering some to Alice first. "It is my mother's famous giblet and sausage stuffing." She placed some standard bread stuffing on the plate before she dug out a chunk of liver and a loop of bowel along with a red chunk of meat that looked somewhat like sausage.

"Sausage? That is sausage? Is it even cooked?"

"Yes, of course it is sausage—blood sausage. It is raw though. We rarely cook our food. We like it fresh. Daddy procured the meat just last night. I told you he had been able to get us some rare and precious delicacies."

"And what is that? It looks like…"

"Like a butt roast. Yes! Most of Mrs. McAllister was really tough, old meat. But this cut was still plump and tender. You will love it. That is my favorite glaze on the top: brown sugar with cherry and blood sauce."

"Is anything made with animal meat or just vegetables?"

# Shadow's Gate

"No animal meat, no. This is Thanksgiving, the one day a year we have been granted the right to eat our natural diet. There are vegetables like mashed potatoes and green beans. The mashed potatoes were made with fresh butter and cream made from human breast milk from the poor mother down the lane. She sells it to us to supplement her income. The green beans have cracklins made from deep-fried human flesh. Aren't you hungry?"

"Wait, wait, wait! Natural diet? I don't understand. This is not normal. This is not okay. I want to go home."

Alice dissolved into tears as she melted into her seat, shying away from everyone, including her best friend, Bethany.

Bethany looked confused herself.

*Why is Alice scared of us? What did she want to eat today? What did I do wrong?*

Sophia got up from the table and carefully scooped up Alice, returning to her seat to wrap her tightly in her motherly arms.

"Oh, dear Alice. Shh, shh, shh. You are okay. Everything is going to be fine. Darling, do you know who we are? Or I should say, what we are?"

"Noooo," Alice sniffled.

"Have you ever heard someone mention the undead... the reanimated... zombies?"

Alice gasped and pulled away from Sophia's chest, staring up into her eyes with horror.

"Yes! Oh my god! Please don't eat me."

"Relax, sweetheart. No one here is going to eat you. You are Bethany's friend. Zombies, as we are commonly known, first started appearing 50 years ago. At first, the whole situation was difficult on both sides. We are drawn to eat meat— raw meat—

and specifically we are drawn to human bodies. In the early days, there were a lot of senseless deaths on both sides. We ate indiscriminately. Similarly, normal humans were fearful and protective of each other, so they attacked many of us without trying to understand or solve the problem.

Things changed back in 2075 after a lot of lobbying from both sides. A few years before that, an animal-based nutrition product was created that simulated the taste, texture and nutritional benefits of human meat. Finally, they passed the Undead Act of 2065 that made it illegal to murder the undead. Likewise, we are prohibited from killing humans for our own consumption. We are required to eat Inconceivable! Meat products. However, we are allowed to eat human meat once a year on Thanksgiving. There is a special process we must go through in order to obtain it. We thought you knew we were zombies."

"I can't eat this. It's not right. Can I just go home now?"

"Dear, I can make you something else to eat."

"I... I... I am not hungry. Anymore. I just want to go now. I won't tell anyone about you. I swear. Just please let me go home."

"Sweetie, of course you can go home. Whenever you like. This is not a secret. We haven't done anything wrong, so there is no secret you need to hide."

No one had noticed the horrified look on Bethany's face during this whole discourse. Her sobbing finally alerted them to her presence as she jumped up and ran to her room. "I'm sorry, Alice. I thought we were friends. I thought you would understand."

"Can I go say goodbye to Bethany? She has been very kind to me."

# Shadow's Gate

"Of course, Alice. You know the way."

Alice left the room as quickly as she could and ran up the stairs to Bethany's room. She found Bethany curled up on the cushions in her reading nook, crying her heart out. "Please forgive me. I didn't know, and I just can't accept it. At least not right now. I love you. I truly do. You are the first person to care about me and help me. Give me some time. Maybe we can play together outside one day. I have to go now."

"Mmm hmm. Bye, Alice, " Bethany mumbled.

Alice quietly exited the room and headed down the back stairs. She was hoping to leave the house without encountering anyone else. At the first landing, she heard hushed voices below.

"You don't think she figured it out, do you? I told her that we had to obtain our Thanksgiving allotment through a special process. The McAllisters were old. She couldn't possibly have figured out that Albert hunted without a permit, right?"

Alice gasped and quickly turned to run back up the stairs.

Sophia jumped at the noise and ran up the stairs to check the source of it. She found Alice cowering in the hallway.

"Hey there, sweetheart. Did you say goodbye to Bethany? Are you ready to go home now?"

Alice tried to bury her horror as she nodded yes.

"OK. I will walk you home then. It is dark outside, and I can't let you walk alone."

"I'm fine. I... I can do it."

Sophia put her arm firmly around Alice's shoulders and led her down the stairs again. "No worries, dear. I am happy to do it. It won't take me any time at all."

Bethany sulked at home the next few days as she finished her Christmas vacation, bored out of her mind because her friend never came out anymore to play. "Will she ever forgive me, Mom? I miss her."

"I am sure she will. Give her some time. Do you have all your homework done before school starts again tomorrow?"

"There have been quite a few cars at the orphanage lately. Do you know why?"

I know they were trying to organize some special events for the kids during the holiday season. And they are going to have a meet and greet for another adoption day, too. I am sure it is nothing to be concerned about."

"Yes, Mom."

Bethany went up to her room to read until bedtime. Then she took her bath, picked out her outfit for the next day, and crawled into bed. The next morning, she rose early to head to school, hoping to see Alice there on the playground. Unfortunately, Alice was nowhere to be found. When she returned home from school, her mother was waiting for her with a refreshing blood shake.

"I need to talk to you, honey."

"Yes, Mom."

"Sit down, honey," she said soothingly as she patted the couch next to her. "I need to talk to you about Alice."

"What about her? Is something wrong?"

"On the contrary, darling. It is very good news. One of those cars you saw belonged to her new adoptive parents. They did have an adoption day, like I told you, and she found the perfect match. They live in Raleigh, so she will be too far away to visit. She has been busy spending time with them, and they left at lunchtime today for the long drive home. She left this for you."

Sophia held out her hand and opened it to reveal Alice's one treasured belonging. She never went anywhere without that little Strawberry Shortcake figurine. It was the one present she had received when she spent Christmas with the only loving foster parent she had ever been placed with.

"She wanted you to know how much you meant to her."

Bethany started to cry softly but smiled as she rolled the little figurine in her hand and held it up to her nose to smell her sweet strawberry scent.

"Why don't you go do your homework while I finish dinner. Your father managed to obtain another delicacy. I am making your favorite dinner; we are having tender, juvenile filets tonight."

Bethany ran up to her room excitedly and dove into her homework immediately. Sophia returned to the kitchen and closed the curtains in the dining room when she saw the flashing lights of the police outside of the orphanage. It wouldn't do for Bethany to see that. It might inspire questions she didn't have an answer for. At least not one that she would want to hear.

# Sharon Marie Provost

# Savage Nature

***D****amn it! I knew I should have made those "additions" to the drug log last night when I took the ketamine. But fuck! How could I have known that the damned inspector from the state board would be here today?*

"Hello, Dr. Williams. I need to speak to you immediately," she said, pursing her lips as she stared at the doctor, gauging his reaction.

"Jennifer can take you back to start your inspection. She has keys to the drug cabinet and can show you where everything else is located. I have patients right now. I will be done before you finish."

"No, doctor! We must speak now. I WILL be doing an inspection later this afternoon, but there is an urgent matter that must be dealt with first. I need you to have your staff cancel your appointments for the rest of the week. Can you ask them to deal with the clients here first? Then we will meet in your office in a moment."

"But..." Dr. Williams' brow furrowed as she shut him down again.

"Doctor, please. This is non-negotiable. The hospital is being shut down pending the results of this investigation. I really think you would rather that we finish this conversation in private."

"Fine," Dr. Williams relented as he met the worried eyes of his front desk staff. Their eyes darted back to their computer screens, but clearly, they had overheard everything. He suppressed a sigh and asked them to start calling that day's appointments first and then move on to the rest of the week. "Tell them there's a family emergency, and let them know we will call to get them rescheduled as soon as possible," he said as he turned to head back to the treatment area.

He let the technicians know that the inspector from the state board had arrived and shut down the clinic, then asked them to handle the two clients waiting to be seen in the exam rooms.

"Jennifer, I need you to gather all the documentation she will need to look over today. I want her to see we run an efficient, professional operation here."

Dr. Williams walked back to his office and shut the door.

The inspector, who was sitting at his desk, waved him over to the other chair.

*Mighty presumptuous of her to sit at my desk!*

Dr. Williams sighed audibly as he perched on the hard wood chair.

"We have heard some very concerning allegations over the

# Shadow's Gate

past few days. First, we received a call from an anonymous employee concerned about missing controlled drugs and erratic behavior on your part. Then two of your clients called in to file reports with us. One alleged that you were aggressive with him... even going so far as to shove him while making threats. He said that you refused to return his pet until he started to dial the police. The other one alleged that he suspected you might be using drugs or alcohol. He mentioned that you seemed agitated and distracted during his last visit. We take reports like this very seriously."

"Let me guess. Was the first client Daryl Roberts?" Dr. Williams asked as he walked over to pick up a chart off his desk and handed it to the inspector.

"Yes, it was. So, what he said is true?"

Dr. Williams held up his hands in front of his chest defensively. "I never said that. Mr. Roberts is a first-class asshole, a drunk and a well-known animal abuser. We have treated his pets for the past ten years. His wife or son usually bring them in. They always seem very nervous when asked to explain why the pets have cigarette burns, contusions, or broken limbs. It is clear that they are concerned about the pets' welfare, and the pets display loving behavior toward them. However, when Mr. Roberts enters to authorize and pay for their care, the whole room shrinks away from him and appears terrified—humans and animals alike. He only allows the bare minimum to be done."

"I see. Have you reported him to the police or the humane society? And what about this incident he claims occurred at his last appointment, on Wednesday, the 16th?"

"You can call them both. I have filed numerous complaints with the humane society. You can find all the documentation in that folder. They have even taken some pets away from him.

However, he always shows up with a new one. The police were involved the last time the humane society confiscated a pet. He was threatening violence against the animal control officers. And before you ask, yes, I do let them know every time he shows up with a new pet. I continue to provide treatment for the sake of the animals, not him. He has stiffed me more than once, I might add."

"So, what was different on Wednesday then?"

Dr. Williams shook his head in disgust. "Mr. Roberts actually brought the pet in himself this time. This particular pet belonged to his son, who was inconsolable. He threatened to report his father to the police for animal abuse. The dog had severe bruising on its flanks. One of the contusions even had a pattern consistent with the tread on his boots. Upon further examination and radiographs, we diagnosed the dog as having a lung contusion and a broken right front leg. It was also significantly malnourished. When I walked back into the room to discuss the treatment plan, I saw Mr. Roberts kick the dog when it laid its head on his foot. His son began to cry, and he had his fist raised to him when I intervened."

"So what happened then? Why didn't you just call the police at that moment?"

"He turned his anger on me when I told him to stop. He approached me aggressively, shouting that I needed to mind my own business. I passed the dog's leash to one of my assistants and told them to take it back it back to the treatment room. He demanded that I return his dog and wrenched his son's arm, pulling him along as he started after them. I explained that the dog needed urgent treatment. He shouted again that I would not be the one giving that treatment. At that point, I did refuse to return the dog and stated I would be contacting the humane society." Dr, Williams gritted his teeth before continuing.

"He grabbed his son's ear and yelled at him for all the trouble he had caused before turning to threaten my staff and me with harm if I did not return his pet. For the safety of my staff, I acquiesced at that point. I will admit I did lose my temper, and I shoved him and then nearly punched him when he wrenched his son's arm again as he turned to leave. However, I did file a police report detailing *all* that had happened—and then called the humane society, so they could do a welfare check on the pet." Dr. Williams stared down at his feet, embarrassment plain to see on his face.

"I see. I will call to verify all this information. Do the police know you assaulted him?"

"Yes, they do. I was advised that I could be arrested if he decided to press charges, especially since there had been witnesses. They promised to go out to the house to check on his son and warn him to stay away from the clinic. Since his son showed no obvious injuries and refused to file a report, they could only give Mr. Roberts a warning.

"Later, I heard back from the humane society, and Mr. Roberts claimed that the pet had passed away not long after returning home. He blamed me, saying the dog hadn't received proper medical care. I can't prove it, but I think he killed it. It tears me up that his anger toward me might have led to that poor dog's death." Dr. Williams looked away as tears welled in his eyes.

"Who is the other owner that reported me?"

"That was Charles Alexander. He said that he brought his pet to you for an emergency and that you were very distracted and agitated with him. What happened there?"

"Well to be honest, that's another difficult situation. I had just heard back from the humane society about Mr. Roberts' dog, so I will admit I was still distressed. Mr. Alexander's dog arrived bleeding from the nose and mouth. The abdomen was distended, and the pet was having difficulty breathing. I sent my assistant out to obtain a history as we started assessing the dog back in the treatment room."

"Mr. Alexander said the pet had eaten a large block of rodent poison a week earlier, and he had neglected to bring it in then because 'the stupid dog did it to himself.' We attempted to start treatment, but the dog died shortly after it arrived. We could have treated that pet and saved it for very little money if he had brought it in right away. Instead, he let the pet suffer and die terribly. After the experience the previous day with Mr. Roberts, it was troubling to have another pet die that way because of an uncaring owner."

"I understand your frustration, Dr. Williams. I really do. But we must act professionally at all times. We cannot let our personal feelings get the better of us, and we cannot be violent as a matter of law in general. I will have to take this information back to the board to assess our findings. In the meantime, the closure stands for the next week. Further, I do need to perform my inspection and speak to your staff regarding that anonymous employee report we received. I think it best that you either stay in your office or leave for the day if you have someone who can close up. We will be in touch with you in the next few days."

Dr. Williams finished writing up his records for the patients he had seen that day and then locked up his office before leaving for home. He was confident his staff respected him, so he wasn't too concerned about what they would say to

# Shadow's Gate

the inspector. Most likely, the complaint had come from a staff member he had recently dismissed due to her frequent tardiness and poor work ethic. He informed his office manager that he would be spending the next week at his lake house, but he would be available by phone if needed.

*My therapist was so concerned that I might be nearing a breakdown. Well, I found the perfect way to blow off some steam. And now I have the free time this week to enact my plan. That bastard is going to pay! He already went too far, but now he is jeopardizing my livelihood and career as well.*

Dr. Williams stopped off at the hardware store on the way home to pick up the last of the supplies he needed. Then he headed out to the old, abandoned barn down Highway 40 to finish setting up. The special guests for this little party were already waiting there.

*I need to hurry because, knowing Roberts, he will be knee-deep in his first bottle shortly after he gets off work at 5. I can't risk him being too intoxicated.*

He hadn't been lying to the investigator when he'd called Roberts a drunk.

An hour later, Dr. Williams finally had the scene set up just right. He loaded his backpack with the equipment he needed to subdue Roberts and left for his lake house. He parked his car in front and ran inside to set the smart home timers so the lights would turn on and off automatically, as if he were in the home. Now that his alibi was set, Dr. Williams got his father's old car out of the garage for the next part of his plan. Roberts lived in a shitty, broken-down mobile home not far from the barn; the closest neighbor was nearly a mile away. He parked the car behind some scrub brush in the field next to Roberts' home. He removed the syringe from the backpack and palmed it. Taking careful steps through the brush to prevent detection, he made his way to the shed and peered in the window.

Daryl Roberts looked tipsy as he worked on his carpentry in the far corner. Dr. Williams removed the cap from the syringe as he tiptoed through the doorway. He wrapped his arm around his target's head, covering his eyes, as he injected the ketamine into his neck vein. Soon, Daryl lost his footing and slumped into Dr. Williams' arms.

The confusion and drowsiness, exacerbated by the alcohol, made him very compliant. Dr. Williams dropped his body into the wheelbarrow and used it to transport him back to the car. He applied a blindfold and tied his client's arms and legs together before stowing him in the trunk.

He returned the wheelbarrow to the shed and made sure he'd left no signs of a struggle, before he returned to the car. Dr. Williams drove back to the barn, propping open the big doors, so he could hide the car inside. He opened the trunk to find Daryl flailing inside.

"I'm flying! I'm flying! But dear God, I've gone blind. Help! Help!"

"Shut up, you idiot," Dr. Williams growled as he jerked him out of the trunk and dropped him on the dirt floor.

He grabbed him by the shirt collar and dragged him into the stall he had prepared. He had chosen to use ketamine because of its amnestic effects. If he could keep it at the right level, Daryl would have no memory of the next few days. With any luck, he may have terrifying hallucinations as well. However, he needed to get him adequately restrained before he woke up enough to recognize his abductor.

Dr. Williams used the tie-down rings in the stall to secure Daryl in place. After helping him drink some water, he replaced the blindfold with a gunny sack tied securely around his neck to prevent him from slipping it off. His pupils were so dilated, and he was experiencing rapid eye movement, so he couldn't have recognized the doctor, even if he had tried.

It was time to bring in the first two special guests to visit their guest of honor. Dr. Williams went to another stall in the back of the barn to retrieve them, leading one by a rope leash and carried the other in a cage. A barn cat had been left behind when the owner of the place lost the property over a year earlier. And Dr. Williams had noticed a few months ago that a stray dog had taken up residence there as well. They subsisted off the rodents in the area, but both were very skinny and hungry. He had reported them to the local animal control office, but nothing had been done to capture them. Now they could have a warm meal.

*After all, animals have been known to nibble on the tasty, tender bits, such as noses, ears and eyelids of their owners, when the owners have been unconscious or dead.*

Dr. Williams smeared some tuna juice across exposed pieces of his captive's flesh. Then he turned the animals loose and walked away to watch via the camera system he had set up earlier. The animals were very nervous at first, avoiding each other and the person on the floor.

Over time, however, their hunger overcame their timidity.

The cat drifted over first and began licking Daryl's fingers. Licking became nibbling. Nibbling devolved into gnawing. The smell of fresh blood and *food* was more than the dog could handle. He stationed himself at Daryl's toes and began to gnaw as well. The pain-control effects of the ketamine dulled Daryl's senses at first, but as they gnawed deeper, he began to stir.

It was time for the next dose of ketamine. Besides, he couldn't let them get too carried away; several guests were left, waiting to visit with Daryl. The two animals ran from the body when he re-entered the stall. He caught them and then released them outside, where more food awaited. He injected the next dose of ketamine and then applied pressure to the wounds to staunch the flow of blood. Daryl's body needed a break, and it was time for Dr. Williams to get some sleep before he introduced the next special guest.

When Dr. Williams rose in the morning, he found Daryl hallucinating that he didn't have arms and legs. This was natural, since he couldn't move them and numbness had set in overnight. Dr. Williams untied them one at a time and moved them around to restore adequate blood flow before injecting him with the next dose of ketamine. When the drowsiness and confusion set in, he untied him to drag him back to another stall set up for the next special guest. He pulled him up onto a chair and tied him in place, so he couldn't fall off. Dr. Williams applied tourniquets to both thighs before he lifted the man's lower legs and placed them in a large, metal trough filled with water.

"You are in luck today, Daryl. I have arranged a special treat for you, a fish pedicure. They are outlawed in the U.S. Then again, this kind shouldn't be legal anywhere."

Dr. Williams laughed as the fish began to swarm around Daryl's feet, removing chunks of flesh from his already mangled feet.

"It is not very easy to get piranhas imported. But if you are motivated enough, you can find just about anything on the internet. I have been planning this for a long time. I didn't think I would ever actually do it, but then you gave me just the motivation I needed to quit being such a pansy."

Dr. Williams stepped behind him and removed the sack

# Shadow's Gate

from his head. He used duct tape to secure Daryl's head to the chair, so he couldn't turn around and see him. The vision of the feeding frenzy before him... on him... was horrifying enough, but the hallucinations only intensified his fear. Soon the water was red with his blood, and Daryl had passed out. Dr. Williams removed Daryl's feet from the water. Only ragged chunks of flesh, loosely attached, remained on his feet. Most of the toes hung loosely from bits of sinew and ligaments still attached to the bones. The small amount of muscle left was torn and oozing.

Dr. Williams applied pressure bandages to stanch the flow of blood. He took him back to his stall and tied him back up. He reapplied the blindfold this time and left him to wake up alone.

Dr. Williams wanted to take his time, so Daryl spent the next two days in a drugged haze. Meanwhile, Dr. Williams cemented his alibi by spending time in Aurora, the small town near his lake house. He was seen throughout town eating lunch one day and dinner the next. He went grocery shopping. He even ran into one of his neighbors while strolling through the shopping district and invited her over for dinner in three days. Dr. Williams was a busy man, splitting his time between Aurora and "caring" for his "friend," Daryl Roberts, at the barn. Right on time, when he returned to the barn late on the second day, he found that an infection had set in on Daryl's feet. It was now time for the next special guest.

*This will all be over tomorrow morning when I introduce the last guest.*

Dr. Williams walked back to open the terrarium, located in another stall. He lifted the small piece of wood on the bottom and found them wriggling underneath on the carcass of a little wood mouse. He carried the terrarium back to Daryl and placed it between his feet. Using a wood tongue depressor, he transferred the maggots from the mouse to Daryl's feet. They began burrowing into the flesh, feasting as they went. He injected Daryl with more ketamine and waited for the hallucinations to begin. His legs twitched as he felt the tickling movements of the maggots across his flesh.

Dr. Williams propped up Daryl's legs on a wood crate. Then he donned a ski mask before removing his captive's blindfold. His eyes grew wide as he saw the small creatures eating him. His screams echoed long into the night as his brain produced all manner of wild visions.

Dr. Williams slept in the car to help dampen the noises Daryl was making.

He rose early the next morning, long before sunrise, in order to set up his last method of torture. This one was straight out of the annals of horrific medieval torture and put Dr. Williams at most risk of being caught. He gave Daryl his final dose of ketamine and loaded him back into the trunk with duct tape over his mouth. It was imperative that Daryl be kept quiet until the last moment.

He retrieved the cage of his most prized special guests and a few other items he had obtained from the hardware store and began the short drive over to Daryl's house.

He drove into the deep brush about a quarter-mile from his mobile home. He put on rubber gloves for this last step to make sure he left no fingerprints. He used a large rubber mallet to drive four tent stakes deep into the ground and knotted ropes onto each of them. He removed Daryl from the trunk and tied him down tight with those ropes, so he could barely move. He placed a heavy metal box over his abdomen. He brought the small cage over and removed the rats one-by-one, which he placed underneath the metal box along with two lit cans of Sterno. Then he weighed the box down with a brick.

# Shadow's Gate

The metal box heated up quickly, and he could hear the rats' nails as they scratched at the sides frantically. But it wasn't long before they found a much *softer* surface to breach for escape. Dr. Williams put his ski mask back on before he removed Daryl's blindfold and the duct tape covering his mouth. He returned to the car before Daryl's screams started echoing throughout the area, leading to the discovery of his mangled body, somehow still clinging to life.

Dr. Williams drove out to a recreation area on the shore of the lake near his home. He changed into his warmup suit in the restroom and began jogging around the lake. Like clockwork, he ran into another of his neighbors who lived across the lake from him. They exchanged pleasantries about the weather, how the town of Aurora had grown, and their shared passion for jogging. Dr. Williams invited him to join him and the neighbor he'd run into while shopping for dinner that night at his house at 6 p.m.

Dr. Williams returned to his lake home after his jog and enjoyed a much-needed shower. The rest of the day was spent puttering about the house, cleaning; doing some minor yardwork; and then preparing for dinner.

He received a call about 4 p.m. from the Police Department back in Gentryville asking for his whereabouts and whether he had seen Daryl Roberts lately. He explained that he had been out in Aurora at his lake house for the past week while he had some time off work. He told him that he had not seen Mr. Roberts since the day he filed the police report because of the threats Mr. Roberts had made. The police thanked him for his cooperation and said they might be in touch again in the future.

His neighbors arrived for dinner right on time. The three of them enjoyed a delicious meal of roast duck, fingerling potatoes, and grilled asparagus.

# Sharon Marie Provost

A rousing game of *Would You Rather* was interrupted by a knock at the door. Dr. Williams re-entered the room, followed by a pair of detectives. He was once again asked about his whereabouts the previous four days. He repeated his earlier statement about being there at the lake house. He looked over at his neighbors, who both readily stated that they had run into him over the course of the week and seen him at home every night. He even produced receipts showing he had been shopping and dining in town throughout the week. They once again asked if he had seen Daryl Roberts recently.

"The last time I saw him was the 15th, when I filed the police report with you guys. He had threatened my staff and me when I refused to return the dog he had abused, and then he abused his son right in front of us. What is this all about? What has he done now? Should I be concerned?"

"Mr. Williams..."

"*Dr.* Williams."

"Yes, I'm sorry. Dr. Williams, he was found early this morning near his home. He had been tortured. He is at St. Mary's Hospital in critical condition, and it is not known if he will survive."

"Oh my God! Do you know who did it? I didn't like the man. I was afraid of him, to be honest. But no one deserves to be brutally attacked."

"No, sir. We are talking to everyone who has had dealings with him lately, trying to figure that out. I appreciate your time. I am sorry we disturbed your dinner party. Here's my card... if you think of anything."

"Yes, detective. Thank you. Have a good evening. Good luck with your investigation. I hope you find the animal that did this."

# Shadow's Gate

"Animal, huh?"

"What else can you call someone who tortures and kills another living creature?"

Dr. Williams returned to Gentryville two days later after receiving a call from the state veterinary board.

"Dr. Williams, we verified all the information you gave us concerning your dealings with Mr. Roberts, including the police report, humane society reports and your own medical records. All of the documentation, and your staff, backed up everything you said. The inspection of your hospital found no areas of concern other than some inconsistencies in the quantities of several controlled drugs, specifically those most likely to be abused. However, your employee, Jennifer, showed us the documentation that your practice had gathered that a certain employee, who was recently terminated, was always on duty and had access to those drugs all the instances when discrepancies were noted. We also found the report you had made with the board regarding this employee and your concerns."

"Yes, all of that is correct. As I told you, I run a tight ship. I regret my behavior when it came to the dealings with Mr. Roberts and Mr. Alexander. It is not an excuse, but I have been under a lot of stress lately. I have a couple of close family members recently. Then there was the employee you mentioned. All I can say is, it all got to me, and I lost my cool. I won't let it happen again. I can promise that."

"That is correct. You cannot let this happen again... ever. We are going to let you re-open Monday. However, we are requiring that you get drug tested weekly for the next six months, since we cannot prove who took the drugs. Likewise, you will need to send in your hospital's drug logs monthly to make sure no further discrepancies are noted. We are also requiring you to attend anger management classes."

"Thank you so much. I really appreciate it. I have started working to develop coping strategies. I was already seeing a therapist to deal with my stress and grief the past few months. She is helping me find ways to blow off steam and relaxation strategies. I already feel much better after this week off. A vacation was just what I needed."

Shadow's Gate

# The Grandfather Paradox

*I can't get her out of my mind. This obsession is patently ridiculous. She is quite literally out of my league... unattainable...*

*So, why can't I get her out of my mind?*

*You know why, you fool! The descriptions of her beauty and allure, comparing her to Aphrodite, Helen of Troy or Cleopatra, pale in comparison to reality. She is quite simply the most beautiful, desirable and impressive woman I've ever seen.*

*She was the belle of the town. Her desirability, though, was her downfall. Every man wanted her, and one greedy asshole decided she*

# Sharon Marie Provost

*shouldn't live if he couldn't have her. I've seen the photos from her funeral. The entire town showed up... the procession was enormous... just as the way it was for Julia Bulette, that other famous 'soiled dove' from Virginia City. If only I could find a way back, everything would be different.*

Will set aside the last known picture of Caroline, taken at the 1874 Fourth of July parade in the old mining town of Pizen Gulch. She had been murdered the following day. Will had tenure as a professor of history, specializing in the Old West, at Arizona State University, but he was on sabbatical to write "the definitive" volume on the soiled doves—prostitutes—of the Old West.

They had entered the world's oldest profession for a variety of reasons. Some had lost their fathers or husbands, and therefore their only means of support. Others had traveled to the Old West in search of adventure—only to find no other means to support themselves. Some were savvy entrepreneurs who entered the profession deliberately in hopes of becoming madams and therefore women of means, if not society.

Saddest of all, though, were the stories of those who were sold into the sex trade and mercilessly exploited, such as Chinese women who had no means of supporting themselves. But even back then, some women just enjoyed the seedier side of life—drinking, dancing and having sex.

Caroline's story was particularly tragic. She had grown up in society in San Francisco until her teens, when her father moved the family out to Arizona Territory following the Gold Rush. Tragedy struck in 1864 when, at the tender age of 15, her parents were attacked and killed by Apaches. She had been left home in the care of her uncle while they traveled to check out a new mine farther to the southwest.

# Shadow's Gate

The family estate, likewise, had been left in the care of her uncle.

A notorious gambler, he had been much too busy with his own affairs to care for a young girl, so she was sent off to a girls' school in town. That is, until he stopped paying for her room and board three months later, at which point she was turned out into the street.

He didn't even bother to pick her up.

The local madam spotted her begging on the street and quickly recruited the naive, desperate young girl, promising her a "service" job at a gentlemen's club. Caroline didn't realize until too late that "service" did not mean serving meals, and that these gentlemen were not the kind she was accustomed to back in San Francisco society.

Her story, although sad, was not uncommon, so she should have just been another chapter in his book. Except she was different: He became so enamored with her photos that he couldn't get her out of his mind. This led to weeks of intensive research, poring over every document he could find that related to the famous Caroline Davis. She was remembered as much for her beauty and kind nature as she was for her brutal murder and the intense mourning that followed.

The murder had occurred on July 5, 1874, in her room at the Overland Hotel. She had been stabbed 18 times in the neck and chest. In the killer's frenzy, blood had been splattered all over the room.

The murderer had never been identified. Several suitors were known to be particularly possessive of her, including two newcomers who had arrived in town during the weeks before her murder. One was simply known as Wilbur, and the other was William Townsend. Both had been seen in her company in the days leading up to the event. Rumors abound in a small town like that, so some people even suspected the less-than-scrupulous sheriff, Robert Atwater, purportedly her favorite suitor. He was known to dispense vigilante justice more often than following the letter of the law. People had been known to disappear, never to be seen again, after having been under the watchful eye of the law. Despite his thorough research Will couldn't get any closer to solving the murder than the investigators had back then.

As his obsession with Caroline and her murder grew, Will found himself contemplating the possibility of time travel. Was there any way to stop her from being killed? But it was more than that. It wasn't just a selfless crusade: He realized, as improbable as it seemed, that he was falling in love with her.

He had always been an open-minded, liberal person who didn't discount any supernatural, paranormal or metaphysical study. However, he hadn't found any theory grounded in research to validate it. Even if he could find a way to get back to her time, it seemed unlikely that he would be able to return himself, let alone bring her back with him. And while he loved studying the Old West, it was an entirely different proposition to contemplate living there for the rest of his life.

Even with all of these issues against him, he found himself studying the history of Pizen Gulch. The town had been created as a stop along the stage line that supplied other nearby mining towns. Whether he stayed there a matter of days, weeks, or for the rest of his life, he would need money... a lot of it... to buy Caroline's way out of that life. To his delight, he found detailed information about the location of a new strike in the area made just prior to her murder. Different sources cited different days, but he would have the money, just in time to convince her. If he could find a way there at precisely the right time, he could provide a comfortable life for the two of them. They could even move on to the next mining boom, in the Black Hills of Dakota Territory in 1875. Then he would definitely have enough money to buy her way back into society in San Francisco.

As his plan took shape, Will redoubled his efforts to find a way to travel back in time. He contacted every expert in the private sector and university research programs he could find. He talked to physicists, astrophysicists, NASA scientists—even educators from the IMHS Metaphysics Institute, Stanford, Duke, Princeton, and Harvard. Some laughed at him. Others doubted the possibility of time travel, but were still trying to find a way. Others still believed that time travel was a given, and it was only a matter of time before people did it regularly.

But even then, there were red flags. Some scientists believed that time travel would only be possible to the future. The theory of relativity, which had been proved reliable many times, seemed to eliminate the possibility of going backward in time.

Of all the potential difficulties, Will found the so-called grandfather paradox most troubling. It postulated that if a person went back in time and killed his grandfather to prevent his own birth, events would simply adjust themselves so that the event would still happen—just not in the exact same way as before. In the simplest terms, if the traveler eliminated his own existence by killing his grandfather, then he wouldn't be alive in the future in order to travel back in time to kill his grandfather.

The grandfather paradox, if true, would make his journey fruitless: Even if he could find Carolina and save her from the original killer, she might still end up murdered by someone else or killed in a different way.

# Sharon Marie Provost

As the end of his sabbatical loomed ever closer, Will set aside all his research on time travel, mining booms, and, more importantly, Caroline, to resume writing his book. Then, two weeks before the deadline, he received an interesting email from one of the astrophysicists he had tried to contact. The man, a Dr. Charles Oberton, invited Will to come see him at the University of Connecticut to discuss his findings.

Will left the email in his inbox unanswered, determined to finish his book and get on with his life. However, he finished his first draft a week ahead of schedule and decided to look over it one final time before sending it off to the editor.

As he came to the chapter on Caroline, he found he couldn't let her go for good until he explored this one last resource. Having found a seat available on a reasonably priced flight out of Phoenix, he logged into his email and sent a response to Dr. Oberton asking if he could meet him in two days' time. He went to put the kettle on for tea and was surprised to find a response when he came back—a response not only agreeing to the visit but inviting him to stay at the doctor's home and offering to pick him up at the airport.

Will booked his flight immediately, only stopping long enough to turn off the kettle. He then returned the email giving Dr. Oberton the specifics about his flight. He knew that if the doctor gave him the information he sought, there would be no better time to pursue his goal than the present. With that in mind, he began to pack items he would need for his meeting with Dr. Oberton, as well as money and clothing befitting a "miner" in the 1870s. Over the past several months, he had been collecting period clothing, coins, and currency from antique stores and online dealers. He called his editor and informed him that he would be unreachable for the next week, but he would be in contact when he returned to go over his changes.

The next few days passed in a blur of activity as he reviewed his preparations over and over, making sure every step was proper down to the finest detail. In an attempt to steel himself against possible failure, he contacted his supervisor at the university to find out what, if anything, he needed to do before his return to the history department. He even left his cat with his neighbor, the local "cat lady," to ensure its care should he not return. Finally, he felt ready to face whatever eventuality might come... except for how to deal with the heartbreak should it not work out.

Will woke the day of the flight anxious about what information Dr. Oberton might have for him. He wasn't sure though if the anxiety would abate if he found out time travel was possible. There were so many variables he couldn't account for, but he knew he had to find out one way or the other. The obsession was eating him alive; he had barely touched any food in several days.

The flight passed quickly with no incidents, and he found Dr. Oberton with ease waiting for him outside the airport. The man certainly fit the appearance of an astrophysicist. He was a short man, dressed in gray slacks with a pinstripe button-down dress shirt under a gray sweater vest. He wore wire-rimmed Coke bottle glasses on his round face, with a mustache and a ring of hair on the sides of his balding head.

"Uh... welcome... welcome, Mr. Andrews."

"Will is fine."

"Yes... yes, Will then. It is very nice to meet you. I have much to tell you. This is all very exciting. I know time travel is possible, but the mainstream science community won't listen to me, even though I have done it myself. A tricky thing it is. But you seemed so motivated when you sent me your message. You unabashedly asked for the so-called impossible... no reticence. I admire that. I know... I just *know* you are the right man to share my knowledge with."

Will struggled to keep up with what Oberton was saying, as the words came out in one long stream of consciousness, no breaths in between, the excitement clear in his words and tone. Will could only respond, "I see," as his mind tried to process all he was hearing.

"I apologize," Oberton said. "I am just so excited. Here... l will leave you to your thoughts until we get to the house, and you get settled."

The rest of the 30-minute drive passed in silence. Will realized that while his anxiety hadn't decreased, his excitement was only rising.

At last, they pulled up in front of a white Victorian home, badly in need of paint and minor repairs. The yard was a jungle of overgrown rose and azalea bushes. Following Oberton, he threaded his way up the narrow sidewalk and onto the porch, taking care not to catch his shirt on the thorns from the roses. It was obvious this man spent most of his time on research rather than caring for his old but otherwise lovely home.

Dr. Oberton showed him to his room, a small affair with a full bed, small bedside dresser and lamp, and a single chair. Interior decorating was obviously not the doctor's forte, either. Dr. Oberton stared at him for a few seconds before turning to leave, "I will let you get settled here. You can find me in my office at the end of the hall to the left when you are ready."

"Thank you. I shall not be long."

Will set his suitcase and duffel bag next to the small closet, then sat on the bed for a moment to gather his thoughts. He wanted to believe, more than he had ever wanted anything before, that the doctor had the answer.

*Seriously! This guy could be a quack. He said no one in the scientific community believes him. That is definitely not a good sign. He can't even care for his home. Does that mean all his energy is devoted to his research? Or is he off his rocker? I can't put this off any longer. I need to go find out.*

Will proceeded down the hall and knocked on the partially closed door at the end of the hall.

"Come in."

Will entered to find an office that looked like it belonged on an episode of *Hoarders*. Every available surface was covered in stacks of papers, tablets, scientific journals, and who knew what else. Dirty plates were stacked on top of it all. In the corner, he saw a chalkboard covered in complicated math equations. He had expected to find a top-of-the-line, state-of-the-art computer system, but instead it looked like it had been purchased in the early 2000s. He looked over to Dr. Oberton to see him hurriedly cleaning off a chair for Will to sit on near the desk.

"Please, please, have a seat, Mr. Andrews... I mean Will."

"Thank you."

Will tried to maintain eye contact with the doctor, but he couldn't stop his head from swiveling around the room surveying it, wondering if a tornado had come through at some point.

"I know. This is not quite what you expected to see, I imagine. Maybe I should have taken you to my office at the university. I have a teaching assistant who keeps everything organized and looking proper there. All my equipment and my main computer are there as well. This is just my old home system. I rarely need a computer here. My home office is more my think tank than a research area."

"Well, to be honest, you are correct. I was a bit surprised. Given that the scientific community at large agrees that time travel is currently impossible—and may well be impossible altogether—I thought your discovery would involve some complicated machinery or device. That you might at least need a computer to show me simulations or something."

"A time machine?" Dr. Oberton inquired with a smirk on his face.

"Well no... yes... maybe... I really don't know."

"I understand your thoughts completely," he said as he pushed his glasses up on his nose, staring intently at Will. "What I tell you might sound utterly fantastical to you. You might even think me crazy when I am finished. I understand if you do. I will not take offense. I only ask that you hear me out. You have nothing to lose, except a little time, but as you told me in your email, your week is free anyhow. As you stated, no one else can offer you time travel now... or possibly ever. I encourage you to keep an open mind and try what I suggest. All you will lose is a little more time and maybe a tiny bit of pride. But what you can gain—only you can tell me what that is—but your face says it is something priceless."

"I must say, you have a very compelling argument there. Okay. I promise to keep an open mind. Shall we get started then?"

"Yes. To get to the heart of the matter quickly—no special equipment is needed in order to time travel—no time machines, computers or any other electrical device. All of that truly is a part of science fiction."

"I don't understand then."

"Think more along the lines of the power of the mind.

# Shadow's Gate

During the Cold War, the government initiated a secret program called the Stargate Project to study psychic phenomena, such as ESP, psychokinesis and remote viewing. The project was eventually terminated, and the official party line declared it a failure, citing a lack of documented actionable intel. But as the average citizen knows, our government lies and hides information from us all the time."

"Then why hasn't some whistleblower come forward?"

"The simple answer: Most whistleblowers don't *truly* give a shit about psychic phenomena. It's not a priority. They come forward about information that affects our health and safety and way of life. The American public, on the other hand, is fascinated with the paranormal and psychic phenomena. That's why shows like *Ghost Adventures, Most Haunted Places in America,* and *Dead Files* are so popular. But they prefer to be entertained, rather than learn the facts."

"So then how did you come to find out about it?"

"I am an astrophysicist, as you know, so I am interested in real, true hard science, verifiable through research, mathematics, and the laws of physics. But I am that rare breed of scientist who is also interested in the supernatural... the paranormal... the existence of true psychic phenomena. Most of this you see around the room—that is my unofficial hobby research into that which cannot be proven... yet.

"When the Stargate Project was shut down in the '90s, I never believed that the project was an abject failure. They never said they had obtained zero evidence. In fact, they said, and I quote, "a statistically significant effect has been observed in the laboratory," yet they still questioned whether psychic phenomena had been demonstrated. That is patently absurd if you ask me. The length of the study—if it ever even truly ended—told me that there was a lot more to the story. So I went straight to the horse's mouth: I sought out as many of the retired scientists from the project as I could find. Most wouldn't talk to me—citing a breach of their non-disclosure agreement and/or classified information—but others could see my genuine interest and desire to delve into the subject more.

"Over time, they came to trust me more and give me more details about their experiments. Dr. Simons, I will call him, finally broke down and told me about time travel; a highly classified and controversial aspect of their research. It requires an intense amount of concentration, discipline and mental/emotional stability. They had achieved it, but the psychological side effects experienced by the travelers were intense. The research was set aside until more safeguards could be put in place for the travelers. He left the program around that time, so he doesn't know where it stands right now. I am sure that they must have tried to change certain events from the past, but he never told me about their success... or failure."

"This is absolutely fascinating, Dr. Oberton. I never knew about that program. So how does time travel work then?"

"That is not surprising. Few people heard about it, even when it was shut down in 1995. It made the TV news, but the story was glossed over and saved for the end of the broadcast. Add that to America's general disinterest, and it was overall a non-story, just as they hoped.

"Time travel involves strictly the power of the mind. One must enter a deep meditative state. It helps, but it is not essential, for you to be at or very near the location you wish to travel to because it helps hone your focus while transporting yourself. During that meditative state, you are in a place of sensory deprivation, so you are not distracted by outside noises, sights, smells, or other stimuli. If you will require proper attire, currency, or any other supply befitting the location to which you are traveling, you must wear those clothes and carry any other items on your person. You can neither take with you, nor bring back, any item or person by merely touching or holding it."

Will realized how lucky he was that he had thought ahead to obtain and pack the appropriate clothing and money that was used in the 1870s.

"How can you be sure that time travel is possible? You said the scientist was retired, so I am assuming he was an older gentleman. Could he be senile?" Will asked as he avoided eye contact.

"I know because I have done it myself... once."

"Why only once?"

"As I told you, it has very serious psychological and therefore emotional effects. I had a nervous breakdown when I returned. But the journey itself was amazing... everything I imagined and more. People are inevitably drawn to change the past, but it never goes well. It never goes as you plan. That can be very hard to handle. It was for me.

"I don't know your plans. You haven't explained to me why time travel is important to you. I don't know whether you wish to travel to the future. I think that may be difficult, if not impossible, since you must be able to imagine and prepare for where you are going. And If you are going into the past, I don't know if you intend to try to change it. If you are, I can't stop you. I'm not going to give you a psychological assessment to determine your fitness for handling the inevitable letdown. All I can do is warn you, and let the chips fall where they may. When someone has gone to the ends of the earth to pursue their dream, I think they should have the right to try. That is why I am helping you."

"Will you tell me about your experience? And if I do this, how do I get back?"

"No, that is something I will not do. Overall, it was much too traumatic an experience for me. I don't wish to feel that pain again. If you want to experience the past... see what things were like, then do it. You will have the time of your life. Just don't fall into that trap of wanting to change it. As far as getting home again, that is surprisingly simple. You are from this world... this time period. Your body and spirit are naturally drawn to your place in time. You will simply meditate once again while thinking about your life here. In a blink, you will return home."

"Thank you, Dr. Oberton. My mind is spinning. I will have to think about everything you said. This is a lot to process."

"Believe me, I understand. This all must seem so contradictory to you. How can I be so excited about time travel, yet not want to travel again myself, having described my journey as traumatic? It is complicated. The scientific ramifications are on a grand scale that can't be quantified... yet. If one can resist the natural human desire to control everything, then time travel is a marvelous experience. It is just not for me. I admit I am weak, and, as a scientist, curious by nature to see what might happen if I tweak this one little thing. You deserved the right to have the knowledge and make your own decision. Now I leave it to you to decide if time travel is right for you. You look exhausted, Mr.... er... I mean Will. Why don't you go rest for a while, and I will have dinner delivered at 6 p.m."

Will had to admit a million thoughts were swirling through his mind. His lighthearted parting with Dr. Oberton before returning to his room belied the weight of his true

# Shadow's Gate

feelings. While he did feel an immense sense of relief knowing that he could reach Caroline; the tension in his forehead and throughout his body broadcast how he really felt.

*That damn grandfather paradox! That must be what Dr. Oberton was referring to when he said the past cannot be changed. But maybe he went about it wrong. He won't tell me what he tried to do. And the others... maybe they tried to kill Hitler or some grand shit like that. I just want to save one young girl. Her life will not change the fate of the whole world, nor will my departure from this time period. I can carefully tailor my successes in the mining booms and our life so that we don't significantly change history.*

The throbbing in his head became overwhelming, so he lay down. His eyes had barely closed before he fell into a deep slumber. He woke an hour and half later to a gentle knocking at the door.

"Dinner is served, Will. Turn left when you exit the room, and when you get into the living room, turn right into the dining room."

"I'll be right out."

Will sat up, relieved to find his headache had gone away. He exited the room and found the bathroom just down the hall. He smoothed his mussed hair and washed his hands before dinner. He walked down the hall and found Dr. Oberton sitting at the dining table with KFC laid out on the table before him.

*I should have known. He is probably utterly dependent on Uber Eats.*

Will took a seat at the table and began to dish up his food. He felt unsure what to say to Dr. Oberton. He knew that the professor was curious as to his reasons for wanting to time travel, but he didn't want anyone to know. He looked up to thank his host for his hospitality and met his curious gaze.

*I knew it. Here it comes.*

"So have you made up your mind? Are you going to try it?"

"Yes, I am."

"Umm... I hope I am not being too nosy. Can I ask where and when—and why?"

"I am going to Pizen Gulch, Arizona, in the 1870s."

"Ohh... how utterly fascinating! Why there?"

"There is a lot of history in that area. There was even a big mining boom there during the 1870s. I don't know if I mentioned it, but I am a history professor, specializing in the Old West."

"I see. It sounds like that will be a very valuable and interesting experience for you. I wish you the best. You must tell me all about your experiences when you come back."

"Yeah... uh, sure. No problem," Will faltered.

Dr. Oberton looked concerned, his brow furrowing at Will's hesitation, but he let the matter go. "So how soon are you going? You going to use the last few days of your vacation?"

"Tomorrow. I am going to book the first flight out in the morning to Tucson and then rent a car for the long drive to Pizen Gulch. I will have an Uber take me to the airport, so you don't have to get up early. I appreciate all you have done for me already. What can I do to compensate you?"

"Nothing, Will. I am happy I could help. Information of this kind should be shared with those who care to know. Just promise me that you will take care of yourself. And of course, I would very much love it if you would share your experiences with me."

Will washed the dishes before returning to his room to book his flight, rental car, and room, and to schedule a pickup for the morning. During his research, he had been happy to find that the hotel where Caroline had lived had not only survived the Great Fire of 1890 but was still operating as a hotel. He couldn't believe his luck when he found they had an opening in the very room she had lived... and died in.

He booked himself for three nights. That gave him a couple of days to try to make a successful journey to 1874. If it didn't work out, then he had enough time to get home in time for school on Monday.

He had studied the history of the area as thoroughly as possible. He needed to make sure he arrived approximately four weeks before her murder. The big strike near Pizen Gulch would occur anywhere from two to four days before her murder, so he had time to stake his claim and work it while wooing her. He had obtained enough old currency to make sure he could live comfortably and properly woo Caroline until then. Once he made the strike, he felt certain, she would be sufficiently impressed to feel safe accepting him as her suitor. Then he could make sure to be with her the day of her murder, so he could prevent it. The plan was foolproof... or so he worked to convince himself.

Will rose early and left a thank-you note for Dr. Oberton taped to the front door. His flight back to Arizona and then the drive to Pizen Gulch went without a hitch. He checked in and set about insulating his room from outside stimuli, adding a blanket over the curtains to block out extra light and placing the "Do Not Disturb" sign on the door. He had bought a set of Bluetooth sleep mask white-noise headphones. The device, mounted on a headband, blocked out light and played soothing white noise while acting as a barrier to outside sound.

Despite his preparations, Will's first attempt at meditation did not go as smoothly as he had hoped. He felt like every nerve ending was on fire with anticipation. Before long, that feeling gave way to the need for a bathroom break.

# Sharon Marie Provost

Just after getting settled again, his stomach began to growl with hunger. He threw the pillow across the room in frustration as he rose again. He went downstairs to the restaurant to get dinner. After he ate, he walked down the street to the store to get a couple of snacks and grab a 40 of Budweiser.

He decided that if he went to bed early and slept until 4 a.m., he could rise early and down the beer and snacks. Then he could wait a few hours to take care of any restroom needs before starting his meditation again at 6. The hotel would still be quiet for hours, so that could only help his cause.

Will began to picture the hotel... the way it looked in 1874. The change in light fixtures... the garish red flower print carpeting... the hustle and bustle of prospectors and prostitutes entering and leaving their rooms. He could hear the rattle of stage wheels in the street, and the whinnying of horses and braying of burros. The room was cloyingly warm in the heat of a July day in southern Arizona. The smell of bacon and coffee wafted up the stairs from the restaurant below.

Will couldn't stand the heat anymore, so he sat up—intending to turn down the heater—and opened his eyes as he reached up to remove the sleep mask. Except it wasn't there. He fell off the edge of the bed when he started at the sound of a gunshot outside. Jumping up, he ran to the window and looked out on the street... the street filled with wagons, stagecoaches, miners and people on horseback.

*Oh my, I did it! I'm here!*

Will burst out of his room and ran down the stairs and out onto the boardwalk. He looked up the street and found the saloon that Caroline worked out of, but she was sure to be up in her room here still asleep. She probably did most of her business during the evening. He needed to go get some more clothes

# Shadow's Gate

anyhow. She would not be impressed if he wore the same outfit every single day. Plus, he needed to find out how to stake a claim. Will spent the rest of the afternoon performing those tasks and then stopped for dinner at the restaurant before heading to the saloon.

Will felt like ball of nerves as he approached. He could hear the lively piano music and the stomping feet of the can-can girls all the way down the block. He pushed through the swinging doors to find the saloon full: not even a space available at the bar. His eyes scanned the girls on stage and those lounging on the velvet sofas, waiting for their next patron to take them upstairs. Caroline was nowhere to be found. He sidled up to the bar and ordered a whiskey, asking the bartender, "Is Caroline Davis here tonight?"

"She's here every night. Better get in line if you want time with her," he replied as he pointed to a group of men lined up by the stairs, the other girls ogling them jealously. As he made his way over, he was startled by a sudden volley of catcalls and whistles. He followed everyone's eyes to find Caroline strutting down the stairs, a wide smile on her face. She made her way over to the bar and was presented with a slew of drinks as men dove over to her side.

Will walked over to Caroline and held his hand out. When she placed her own in his, he kissed it and said, "Miss Caroline, it is a pleasure to make your acquaintance. May I buy you a drink?"

Caroline giggled and gave him her hand. "I'll take a whiskey neat. Thank you for asking, Mister...?"

"Pardon me, Miss. My name is Will Andrews."

"Will... short for William, Wilford, Wilbur?"

"Wilbur, Miss. But nobody has called me that since I was ten years old."

"Until now that is... You shall forever be Wilbur to me. I am very pleased to meet you, Wilbur. Care to have a seat with me over there?"

She led him over to one of the sofas in the back corner. Will followed her over, his heart in his throat.

"Thank you, Miss Caroline. Your beauty far exceeds even the most favorable tale I have been told. I have traveled farther than you can imagine for a moment in your presence."

"You are too kind, Wilbur. Don't tell me you came to Pizen Gulch just for l'il ol' me," she drawled with a wink."

"You caught me. I cannot lie to one as fair as you. I was headed to the area to do some prospecting. When I was researching where to go, I kept hearing about Pizen Gulch and its most lovely resident, the fair Caroline. The decision was made for me."

Caroline blushed as she looked down at her hands fidgeting in her lap. "Wilbur, I have to ask, for I feel like you are trying to woo me: Do you know my profession?"

"Yes, Miss, I do. But you cannot blame a man for trying. I can give you a comfortable life now, but if I strike it rich one day I would whisk you away to live in luxury... that is, if you would have me."

"There is one other little issue as well. Sheriff Atwater has been my suitor for the past year. He provides security for me and the other girls. He really has been very kind to me. He, too, says he can provide me with a comfortable life. I wouldn't want to hurt his feelings. Plus, more concerning for you, he's very jealous when any other man tries to steal my heart."

"I understand. I am not afraid of him. I will discuss the issue with him man-to-man if you like."

"Wilbur, I am not the marrying kind. If I were, I would

have accepted Sheriff Atwater's proposal long ago. I have told him this many times, but still, he hopes and waits. I continue our courtship because it is mutually beneficial: It makes him happy, and it keeps me safe."

"Well Miss Caroline, will you accept my friendship and indulge my attempts to court you?"

Caroline looked at the long line of men waiting for her company. She could hear them grumbling about the delay. She stood up abruptly and turned to Will. "I suppose I could try. I really do have to get going though. Pizen Gulch is an expensive place to live, so it is time I earn my living."

"Please wait one moment, Miss Caroline. I would be happy to pay for your company for the whole evening."

Caroline giggled. "You really don't give up, do you? Let's start with you having one potential enemy, why don't we. The sheriff will be enough for you to handle one day after entering town."

"Then, will you do me the honor of meeting me for a late lunch tomorrow? I am staying at the Overland Hotel. I am sure you know they have a lovely restaurant downstairs."

"Yes, Wilbur. I will meet you there at 1 p.m. Good evening, kind sir."

Wilbur returned to the bar to order one more whiskey to celebrate. He had made more progress on the day of his arrival than he ever could have expected. After he finished his drink, he left the saloon, whistling as he returned to his room at the hotel. He forced himself to think about how to win Caroline's heart and secure their future, rather than what she was doing upstairs with those other men. He decided to turn in early because he was exhausted after all he had been through that day. Besides, he needed to get up early to find and stake his claim so he could file it with the mining office. His whole plan was predicated on him being able to support Caroline in the means to which she had once been accustomed.

The next morning, Will was up at dawn and headed out to his mining claim. He staked out the claim and worked on it for a few hours. Afterward, he stopped off at the assay office to have a sample tested and filed the results with the mining office.

As he was walking through town, he noticed some desert wildflowers blooming nearby, so he stopped to collect a small bouquet for Caroline. He ran upstairs to his room and placed them in a pitcher of water while he cleaned up before lunch.

Will headed down to lunch early to secure a coveted table near the window. The flowers were lying on the table, waiting for Caroline's arrival. He was pleased to see her walking down the stairs in what must have been one of her finest outfits; he must be winning her over if she cared to dress up for him. He rushed to the door to meet her, flowers in hand. She smiled that dazzling smile of hers and leaned forward to give him a kiss on the cheek as she accepted them, then he led her to the table and helped her into her chair.

"I have taken the liberty of ordering for us. I hope that is all right with you."

"I suppose. And what are we dining on then?"

"I ordered us both a steak medium rare, a baked potato and vegetables. Or would you prefer something else?"

"No, that is lovely. I can't remember the last time I had a steak."

"Sheriff Atwater doesn't buy you fine dinners?"

"He does what he can. Like I said, he can offer me a comfortable life, but not one filled with luxuries. So, Wilbur, where are you from?"

"Born in California, then Nevada since 1864, until the past

year when I moved to Tucson."

"Where are you from, Caroline?" He knew what her answer would be, but he was careful not to let her know.

"I grew up in San Francisco, where I lived until I was 13. Then my father moved us out here to Arizona to follow the Gold Rush."

"May I ask how you came to... to be...?"

"How I came to be a lady of the night, you mean?"

"Yes. Forgive me. I should never have asked."

"You didn't. Don't worry though. I don't mind. It is the typical story one would expect... so many of us were orphaned or widowed. In my case, I became an orphan at the age of 15."

"Oh my! So young? I wish I could have been there to help you."

"Take advantage of a young girl? Why Wilbur, I thought you more honorable than that."

"Oh no, I never meant that. I would never! I... I just meant..." Wilbur stammered.

Caroline laughed, her eyes twinkling, "I know what you meant. I was teasing."

Will and Caroline spent the next two hours enjoying each other's company. When the waiter came by for the third time asking if they needed anything else, Caroline realized how much time had passed.

"Oh dear, I am late. I really must leave at once. My clientele expects me at the saloon by 2 p.m."

"Caroline, may I buy your time for a few more hours? I enjoyed our time together. I don't want it to end."

"To be honest, I have, too. But I don't want to cause you any trouble. There are some very tough, possessive men in this area. They don't dare quarrel with Sheriff Atwater, but I wouldn't want someone to hurt you. I really must remind you that this is going nowhere... other than friendship. No sense causing yourself trouble needlessly."

"Then may I request your company for an excursion just outside town tomorrow? I want to show you something."

"I suppose so. I live here in the hotel as well. Do you want to meet out front at noon tomorrow?"

"Perfect. I will see you this evening, at least for a moment. I will come down to the saloon for a drink later. Have a pleasant afternoon, Miss Caroline."

Will gently brought her hand to his lips to kiss it once more before walking her to the door.

Will returned to his room in a daze. He couldn't believe how well this was going. The sample from his mine had tested positive for gold. The major strike would be found in a matter of weeks, so he had time to convince her to be his... or at least allow him to be close enough to her to protect her from her attacker. Then they had their whole lives for their love story to play out.

Will decided to stay home that evening... *A little absence makes the heart grow fonder.* The next day he once again left early to work his mine, hoping he might find a gold nugget to present to Caroline. As fortune would have it, he did find a small nugget, which he took to the jeweler to be set in a dainty necklace that he knew would look beautiful on Caroline's long, slender neck. The jeweler said it would be ready that afternoon, so they could pick it up later on the way back into town after visiting the mine.

He stopped by the restaurant to pick up some sandwiches and fruit for a picnic lunch. Then he headed out to the front porch to wait for Caroline to come down. Once again, she descended the stairs exactly on time. She was surprised when a wagon pulled up a moment later to pick them up for the ride out to the mine.

"Are you sure, Wilbur? This must have cost you quite a bit. I am no weakling. I can walk to wherever we might be going."

"It is about a mile and a half away. I am sure you can walk, but you shouldn't have to. Let me spoil you. This is how a lady should be cared for."

"Well, I suppose we could if you are sure."

Will smiled and gave her his hand to help her up into the wagon. They chatted and ate their lunch on the way out to the mine. When they stopped in the mining district, Caroline looked at him quizzically. He helped her out of the wagon and led her over to his claim.

"This claim right here is mine. I took a sample to the assay office yesterday, and it tested positive for gold. I found more today with minimal work. I am going to strike it rich... soon. You'll see. Then I'll be able to support both of us. Take care of you the way you should have been all this time. Will you consider it?"

"I don't know, Wilbur. I told you I am not the marrying kind. I will not be controlled by you... or any other man... ever. This is all happening so fast. I have become accustomed to this life. I must admit I am a happy woman. I am able to see to all my needs. I want for nothing. Besides, I appreciate all the attention from the men in town. It makes a girl feel desired."

"I understand, Caroline. I won't push you. Just promise me you will consider it. I am not going anywhere."

"I promise nothing, but I will think about it. We should head back toward town, so I am not late again today."

"Yes, of course. We have one quick stop on the way back. I promise I will have you back on time."

"Fine, Wilbur."

They chatted about their childhoods and places they had lived. Will was careful to only mention details that were era-appropriate. The conversation was easy and enjoyable for both of them. The ride back passed by in a blink.

Caroline asked where they were going when they stopped at the edge of town. Will jumped off the wagon and held out his hand to help her down. "Over here, " he pointed to the jeweler as he took her hand to lead her over.

"No, Wilbur. I told you."

"Shh shh shh. Relax. You will see in a moment."

Will walked up to the counter. The jeweler greeted him warmly and handed over a small parcel wrapped in brown paper and tied with twine. Will led her back outside to the bench on the porch.

"This is just a small token from me. I hope you like it."

Caroline opened the package, suspicion on her face. However, she couldn't contain her smile when she saw the small heart-shaped pendant and the gold nugget inside. She pulled it out of the box and dangled it in the sunlight.

"Oh, Wilbur! This is gorgeous."

"This is the first nugget from my mine. There is no one I would rather give it to than you. Please say you will accept it."

"Of course! This is the sweetest gift I have ever received. Thank you so much!" she exclaimed as she threw her arms around him, hugging him tight.

When they got back to the saloon, Will helped her out and turned to say goodbye.

"Wilbur, please come by tonight. I would like to spend some time with you. No charge of course."

# Shadow's Gate

"I will come by, but I will be paying you."

Caroline's face fell as she turned to leave. "Of course. You are like all the rest. I'll see you later, Will."

"No, no, no. That is not what I meant. As long as you are not mine, I will not take up your working time without fairly compensating you. We will enjoy a drink and visit downstairs, but I will pay you just the same. I meant it about wanting to support you, one way or the other."

Caroline skipped up the stairs to the saloon, a wide smile on her face. Will walked back out to his mine, eager to strike it big. He found some promising samples that he hid in his room. That night he did visit Caroline, and she set aside two hours for him, even as the miners in line glowered at them. As he rose to leave, Caroline leaned over and kissed him on the cheek. The smile on her face lit up the entire room. Head in the clouds, Will didn't notice Sheriff Atwater scowling as he approached him.

The sheriff stepped out in front of him. "Excuse me! You mind telling me who in the Sam Hill you are? You only rolled into town a few days ago, and you have been spending an awful lot of time with Caroline Davis... my sweetheart, I might add. Just what are your intentions?"

"I have not broken any laws. I am simple miner, like most everyone here. As for my intentions, that is between me and Miss Caroline. I think you may need to ask her yourself, but she told me her heart belongs to no one. In my book, that means I am free to pursue her if I choose. Now pardon me, I was just leaving."

Will attempted to push past the sheriff, but the man was immoveable like a mountain.

Atwater grabbed his collar and dragged him back to face him. "I don't remember saying you could leave yet, Mister... I don't recall you giving me your name."

# Sharon Marie Provost

"Will Andrews."

"I am the sheriff in this here town, and what I say goes. Do you understand that? I told you that Caroline Davis is my girl. You will leave her alone from now on, or you will be sorry. Am I making myself clear? This is a rough town full of rough people, and that includes me. Don't make it any harder on yourself."

Sheriff Atwater shoulder-checked Will hard as he passed by, headed toward Caroline. The million-watt smile had dimmed as her brow furrowed, her eyes darting between the two of them.

The miner who had just sat down with her jumped up to let the sheriff sit down. The two of them began a serious discussion that soon moved upstairs; the sheriff leading her up the stairs, an iron grip on her forearm. Will left the saloon dejected. He had never meant to cause her any distress. Given the current power dynamic though, there was nothing he could do at this moment.

Will returned to the hotel and turned in early for the night. He had a long day of mining ahead of him. The big strike would happen soon. He wouldn't have much time over the next couple of weeks to see Caroline, but it might be best if he let the dust settle anyhow. Besides, his priority needed to be making enough money to get her away from this town—and the sheriff.

The next day, he worked from sunup to sundown. He found more promising samples, which he dropped off at the assay office, then wandered around the outskirts of town searching for a suitable home for Caroline. He knew the boom that was about to hit Pizen Gulch would be large but short-lived. They would have to live here for just under a year. Then they could move to Dakota Territory for the next boom, or she could choose somewhere they might live a comfortable but happy life on the fringes of society. The only things that mattered: She would belong to him and never have to work again.

As he re-entered town just before dinner, he was surprised to see Caroline walking down the street toward the saloon. Normally, she would have been working the saloon for several hours already. She kept her head down, avoiding his eyes, but he could tell she was looking at him. He raised his hand a bit to wave to her, but he noticed the sheriff down the street by the hotel, watching them. He did not want to incite any more trouble, so he adjusted his hat instead.

As she turned to enter the saloon, he noticed the dark bruising under her right eye.

*That fucking asshole hit her! What kind of sheriff is he? With a temper like that, he probably is the one who murdered her. I have to stop this somehow. If I have to kill him myself, she will not be the one to die this time.*

Will ascended the stairs to clean up before dinner. His door was standing slightly ajar—the contents of his room strewn about—although nothing appeared to be missing.

*No mystery who fucked with my room! That fucking sheriff was standing right outside of the hotel. He wanted me to know it was him.*

Will put his room back together, then cleaned up for dinner. He put on a new pair of dungarees and a blue pinstripe shirt. He went down to the restaurant to have a quick meal before going to the saloon to visit her. Even though she wasn't her usual vivacious self, Caroline still held the attention of every man in the room.

Will waited his turn to visit her for a few precious moments that night. She warmed as the evening went by with no trouble.

# Sharon Marie Provost

Will continued to work hard each day and then visit Caroline each night at the saloon for the next few weeks, just like all the other men. Even though their time together was short, it became precious to both of them... neither one of them wasting one single moment.

As the day of the strike approached, Will grew anxious to make the relationship progress. He'd had no other run-ins with Sheriff Atwater, so he decided to begin courting her more seriously. After a hard day working, he stopped to eat dinner and pick up some dessert for later. As he walked down to the saloon, he stopped to gather more flowers for Caroline.

He entered the saloon and found it nearly full. The line for Caroline curved around the corner, filling every seat on the velvet sofas. He bided his time, resolving to stay patient as he drew up a chair to sit next to the last in line.

Caroline met his eyes and couldn't hide her smile.

Five hours later, as the clock was striking midnight, he finally reached the head of the line. He paid her fee, and this time she led him up the stairs. The flowers had begun to wilt, but she fawned over them as if they were the finest bouquet of long-stemmed roses. He presented her with the dessert, and she insisted that they share it to protect her girlish figure. They spent the next hour laughing and teasing each other as she lay with her head on his chest. As the clock neared one, he leaned forward and whispered a sweet nothing in her ear, then placed one chaste kiss on her lips.

Caroline met his kiss hungrily. She wrapped her arms around him and held him tight as he rolled on top of her. He softly kissed each eyelid, her cheeks, the tip of her nose, her forehead; then he met her mouth once more. His eyes found hers, an unspoken request for permission could be seen in them. She nodded, and he caressed her face as they began to make love.

Afterward, they lay in each other's arms for a few moments before he sat up to leave. He knew she had other customers waiting downstairs, and he didn't want to cause her any more problems. He placed one kiss on her face where the bruise had been a few weeks ago and expressed remorse for having been the cause of it, even if it had been indirectly. He reached into his pants pocket to retrieve his wallet, and her hand reached out to stop him.

"Please don't treat me as your whore."

"Caroline, I would never. I could never. I told you I would support you, and I kept you from your customers."

"I chose to spend that extra hour with you. You are not just another paying customer. I feel something for you that I never thought I could or would."

"Caroline, would you…"

"Stop, please. I told you I would consider it. Please don't rush me. The situation is complicated."

"I understand. I would never force you into anything, nor do I want to cause you any more pain or suffering. Is there a back stairway I can use to exit in case the sheriff is here? I wouldn't want him to hurt you again"

"Yes. Turn left when you exit the room, and it is at the end of the hall. Goodnight, dear Wilbur. I lov… I mean I would love to see you again tomorrow."

Caroline turned away quickly, a blush upon her cheeks. He placed one quick kiss on the top of her head and exited before he was overcome. He slipped out and walked in the shadows back to the hotel.

# Sharon Marie Provost

Sheriff Atwater saw the coward slip out the back door just as he had expected. Several of the miners had told him that the filthy newcomer had just gone upstairs with his girl when he arrived. Now, two hours later, he had finally departed.

*I am going to put a stop to this... here and now. After all I have done for her, this is the way she repays me. She promises to consider marriage while she ALLOWS me to court her. She has never been this receptive with me. Fucking whore!*

Sheriff Atwater passed the other miners still waiting for their turn for time with Caroline. Seeing his face purple with anger, no one dared say a word about him cutting in line.

Caroline heard the sound of his feet thundering up the stairs. She opened the door to let him in and cried out when he grabbed her wrist, twisting it as he pushed her back inside the room.

"I won't stand for this any longer. I refuse to let you treat me this way, ignoring all I have done for you. I protect you and all these other girls. You wouldn't be safe to walk these streets at night if it weren't for me. I have taken you out to dinner and bought you gifts, yet still, a year later, you have not accepted my proposal."

"I am sorry, Robert. I have told you that you shouldn't count on me marrying you. I didn't want to accept your gifts because I didn't feel... that way, but you insisted."

"Well, I have a new proposal for you. And this one, I think you will accept: You end things tomorrow with your little lover boy, or I will end his life. I am the law around here. Nobody will question me if I say he attacked me. He is new to this town and no one here even likes him... except for you. Then you will accept my proposal, and we will be married in the fall."

"But..."

# Shadow's Gate

"But nothing. There is no room for negotiation here. What is your answer?"

Caroline felt weak, her knees buckling as she sat on the bed. Her red-rimmed eyes met his, and she nodded her assent.

"That's a good girl," he cooed as he ran his hand across the top of her head. "I will tell the others that you are not seeing anyone else tonight, so come back tomorrow. I am going to have a couple drinks, and then I will walk you back to the hotel. I expect you to be ready to go and happy to see me when I return."

Caroline turned her head when the tears began to flow, as a soft "Yes," tumbled from her lips. The door closed hard. Caroline curled up into a ball on the bed, crying until she felt every drop of moisture had left her body. An hour later, she heard the sheriff's footsteps ascending the stairs, so she wiped her eyes and stood up to smooth her dress. When he entered the room, she dutifully came forward to link her arm in his, so she could lead him to her bed at the hotel.

Caroline knew the night was far from over.

The next day Will returned to his mine, excited by the prospect that this would be his day to strike it rich. Tomorrow was the Fourth of July, and he knew the strike had occurred before the holiday. Better yet, *his* Caroline had nearly told him she loved him. That knowledge gave him the energy to work harder and faster than he ever had before. He'd never performed blue-collar work before, so he had begun his endeavor at a distinct disadvantage when it came to strength and endurance. Even now that he had worked a couple of weeks, he was only starting to get used to it.

The sun was almost touching the horizon when he hit a

large vein of what appeared to be pure gold. He nearly whooped with delight before remembering he was living in the Old West now.

People died over claim disputes or from robberies on the road.

So Will obtained a sample discreetly and stowed it deep in his lunch pail before covering all evidence of the strike. News would get out soon enough when the assay results were leaked. For now, he would hide his discovery until he had obtained enough money to afford some kind of security. He hurried down the road and back into town, hoping to reach the assay office before it closed. It wouldn't be open tomorrow because the town was having a big Fourth of July celebration and parade.

Will dropped off the sample just as the assayer was about to lock the door and was told the results would be available first thing in the morning on the 5th. Will returned to the hotel to eat dinner and go to bed early.

Tomorrow would be a long, exciting day.

Will rose early to get some breakfast before heading out to enjoy the festivities. He knew Caroline would be busy most of the day. She had been chosen to lead the parade and act as hostess for many of the activities. He needed to find a way to get some time with her before the end of the day to arrange to be with her tomorrow. The reports he had read stated that her murder occurred sometime between noon, when she came down to eat, and 3 p.m., when one of the other saloon girls came by to borrow a dress and found her door ajar.

His concentration was broken by the wave of whistles on the road beside him. He looked up to see Caroline riding a wagon, where she was seated on a bale of hay. She was wearing the most beautiful red ball gown, with a large royal blue silk bow tied in her hair—the silken ringlets framing the face that had come to haunt him from that picture in his research. She took his breath away when she turned that smile on him—until seconds later, when it began to falter.

She quickly turned away, to the delight of the miners waiting for her attention. Will couldn't understand why she had stopped smiling when she recognized him. He looked around to see if the sheriff was nearby, but he couldn't find him. He tried to tell himself to relax as he moved on to the day's next activity. But no matter where he saw her, she always seemed to find a way to avoid looking at him or dealing with him—even when she was handing out forks for the pie eating contest or gunny sacks for the two-legged race.

When evening arrived, the festivities moved to the saloon.

Will stopped to get some dinner before making his way down to see her. He headed over to the usual line of men to wait his turn but was told tonight was special: Tickets for her company had been raffled off earlier in the day. He had missed his one and only opportunity to see her.

*I have to find a way to get her a message.*

He sat down at the bar to have a drink... his head in his hands.

Melanie, another saloon girl, stopped over to greet him. "I know you two are in love. Anyone can see it. If you want to write her a note, I will make sure she gets it."

"You would do that?"

"Sure, sweetie. I am a sucker for love."

"This is very important... a matter of life and death you might say. Promise me that she will get it tonight, and that you will make sure she reads it."

"I will, darling. Don't you worry your sweet little mind."

Will hastily scribbled out a note and handed it to her along with money to compensate her for her time. He finished his drink, then returned to the hotel. He tried to wait up for Caroline, but his weariness got to him. He knew he needed to be at his best tomorrow to change her fate, so he climbed into bed.

The next morning he woke late, cursing himself for sleeping in. He rushed down the stairs for brunch and then headed over to the assay office. He needed those results in hand to prove to her that he could care for her.

The assayer's son nearly fell over himself rushing to give Will the news. The sample he had brought in contained the purest gold of any from the surrounding area. He wanted to know where Will had been mining so he could stake his own claim nearby.

Will agreed to let him know the next day if he promised to withhold the information about Will's strike until he was prepared to deal with it.

The young man agreed without hesitation.

Will ran back to the hotel because noon was fast approaching. As he poked his head into the restaurant to search for her, the clerk called out to him from the front desk. He didn't see her, so he walked over to find out what he wanted.

The clerk handed him a note.

"Miss Davis just went back up to her room after eating lunch. She told me I must give you this note as soon as I saw you."

"Thanks."

Will opened it as he dashed up the stairs. His heart raced as he read the words: *I must speak to you as soon as possible. Meet me downstairs at 1:30.*

Will knew he couldn't wait. She could be killed any moment, so he raced to her room and knocked on the door.

Caroline opened the door and gasped as he rushed inside.

"What's wrong? Are you okay? What did you need to discuss?"

"Excuse me! I don't remember inviting you in. In fact, I distinctly remember my note stating I would meet you *downstairs* at 1:30 p.m."

"I apologize. I was just worried that something was wrong. And I was excited... so excited. Look at this, Caroline. I did it! I struck it rich!"

Caroline reached out to take the piece of paper he was holding out. She smiled and handed it back. "I'm very happy for you."

"No, be happy for *us*. I told you that I would strike it rich so I could support us. I will take care of you for the rest of your life, just as you deserve."

His stomach twisted in knots as he saw the look of revulsion on her face. Her sneer seared itself indelibly into his memory as she began to speak.

"Goddammit! Stop it, Wilbur! You don't own me... now or ever. I wouldn't marry you if you were the last man on earth. Your weakness disgusts me. You didn't stand up to the sheriff when he confronted you. He beat me that night because of what *you* said to him. If you care so much about me, why didn't you stand up for my honor when you saw what he had done to me? Then you fucked me the other night and slipped out the back door like a coward... too afraid of what would happen to your own precious self if you were caught. I want a man... a real man... a man like Robert."

"No, you don't mean that. How could you want to be with him? He hurt you."

"He hurt me because of *you*. He has protected me for the last year. He killed a drunk who tried to attack me once. Now *that* is a man. He doesn't beg and plead like a child the way you do. It is not attractive to beg, Wilbur. You are a tenderfoot. You just got lucky finding that gold and you'll never hold that claim. You're weak, Wilbur. Pathetic. Someone will jump that claim and kill you before you can say boo."

"Please stop, Caroline. This isn't you. What happened?" He was dumbfounded, but he could feel something else rising inside of him.

Anger.

Caroline turned toward the mirror, admiring her appearance. "Take a good look, Wilbur. Do you really think I would ever let myself be seen with someone like you? I'm a *lady*, Wilbur. But you? You're ugly enough to back a buzzard off a gut-wagon. Now get out of my sight. I refuse to waste any more time with you."

"Caroline, I love you."

"You are foul. You couldn't pay me enough to let you touch me again. I have scrubbed and scrubbed, and I still don't feel clean."

Will's already red face turned purple. He let out a feral howl of rage. "How dare you! You ungrateful bitch! You don't know what I have done for you." He slid his hands along her vanity, sending the wash basin and pitcher crashing to the floor. He picked up the shiny, silver letter opener and turned to her in a blinding flash. Lunging, he thrust it forward, stabbing her in the neck, plunging the blade deep into her jugular and carotid artery.

# Shadow's Gate

Blood spurted out to cover his face. He slashed the blade across her face, opening a deep gash before plunging into her chest again and again.

Caroline slumped back onto the bed. Her breathing slowed and blood gurgled in her throat, a small rivulet draining from the corner of her mouth. She looked up at Will, pleading with her eyes, as she tried to speak to him.

He leaned over to hear what she said.

"I love... you... Wilbur. Robert said... uhhh... kill you."

Will collapsed onto the bed as she breathed her last breath. He wrapped his arms around her, trying to cover the wounds that only oozed blood now that her heart had stopped beating.

*Oh my fucking God! What have I done? I came here to save her from an unknown killer. Oh no! No! No! No! No! It can't be. That just can't be. I am the killer. I was always the killer.*

Then he remembered what he'd read: One of the men she'd been seen with had been a newcomer to town named Wilbur. He'd disappeared from town around the time of her death.

*Why didn't I ever think about that? How could I have done this to her? I am not a violent man. I have a temper, but I've never lost it like this. I wasn't thinking straight. My head isn't right. Something's... just... off...*

Will slammed his fists on the bed and then slapped his forehead.

*What is wrong with me? How can I make this right?*

*There must be a way to fix it.*

*Wait! If I die here, then I won't be alive in the future to travel back in time to kill her. Right? Right?*

*I have to try.*

*It has to work.*

*It only makes sense. Right?*

# Sharon Marie Provost

Will climbed to his feet and returned to his room. He cleaned himself up and put on the suit he had arrived in before making his way down to the sheriff's office. He was disappointed to find that Sheriff Atwater was out and would not be back until that evening. Will spent the next several hours wandering through town... his mind in a fog of mourning and denial. He knew the sacrifice she had made to protect him, yet he still felt angry at her for what she had said to him. And shame! And regret!

*Am I losing my mind?*

Darkness fell as he rounded the corner of the saloon to head up the alley toward Main Street. He ran directly into Sheriff Atwater.

"I've been looking for you, you sonofabitch!"

The sheriff tackled him throwing bone-crunching punches into his face.

"I'm sorry. I'm so sorry. I didn't mean to. I loved her," Will whined.

"We all loved her, you asshole. I knew you were trouble when I saw you. I should have taken care of you then."

Sheriff Atwater pulled his gun and shot Will three times in the chest.

Will struggled to breathe as his lung collapsed. As his world faded to black, he whispered, "Thank you."

Sheriff Atwater had his deputies help him dispose of the body in an abandoned mine shaft. The town threw the largest funeral anyone had ever seen. The murder was listed as unsolved. It was easier than having to explain the lack of a trial.

Everyone in town knew the truth. Most of them wished that the sheriff had made Will suffer more for taking away their

# Shadow's Gate

"Diamond in the Desert."

Will awoke with a start, his head thundering. He looked around the room, trying to figure out where he was. Then he realized he was lying in the bed at the Overland Hotel, and it all came rushing back to him as he stared at the modern amenities surrounding him.

He curled up in a ball and cried until he was hoarse and could no longer produce tears. He couldn't live with what he had done. He couldn't live without her.

*That fucking grandfather paradox! I did everything right. She should be in my arms now. We should be celebrating our wedding night. How could this have happened? I am not a killer. I loved her more than anyone. But maybe I didn't kill her. Maybe the sheriff stopped it all by killing ME. But then what am I doing back here? Oh God! That means I still killed her... didn't I? If there's any chance I succeeded... I have to check!*

Will rose from the bed. The room was still laid out exactly as it had been back in 1874. The bed was different, but he could still see Caroline lying there, covered in blood. He felt weak, emotionally drained, unable to think clearly.

He made his way out of the room and down the stairs. He remembered that the hotel had a memorial plaque and oil painting of her hanging above the fireplace in the sitting area just off the lobby.

*Please don't be there. Please don't be there!*

Will rounded the corner and was confronted with the memorial just as it had been before. He walked over to the plaque and read the inscription: It still said the exact same thing about her being murdered by an unknown assailant.

*That fucking sheriff must have covered up his own vigilante justice and left the crime listed as unsolved. What a coward! What kind of man hits a woman because he is jealous? He didn't own her. Oh shit! Fuck fuck fuck fuck FUCK! Probably the same kind of asshole that kills her because she breaks up with him... says whatever she has to in order to make him go... so she can save him at her own expense.*

Will walked through the lobby and down the hall into the small technology room at the back of the hotel. There was just one more thing to do: He needed to send that email he had promised.

Will's account of his experience to Dr. Oberton spared no detail. Shame and guilt were his constant companion now... no sense hiding it from the doctor.

He pressed SEND as the tears began to flow again.

He then went back upstairs to his room and put pen to paper: *I loved her with all my heart. I cannot go on without her. Please forgive me.* He left the note on the desk along with his wallet and keys. His phone began to ring, but he pressed the mute button to silence it before placing it next to his wallet. He used the bedsheets to tie a noose and hung himself from the railing on the balcony outside. The drop wasn't long enough, so his neck didn't break. He suffocated slowly, legs kicking, as the image of her bloody body burned itself onto his retinas.

The quiet town of Pizen Gulch didn't notice his body hanging there until two hours later, when the mailman stopped to deliver a package to the front desk.

Dr. Oberton received the email only a minute after Will had sent it. He read it quickly and grabbed the phone to call Will.

There was no answer. He tried again but still no luck.

He called the hotel and had the front desk ring the room, but Will didn't answer that phone either.

The desk clerk told Dr. Oberton that they had seen Will in

the lobby near the exit, so they assumed he had left. Dr. Oberton feared the truth was much darker. He called Will's cell phone once more and left a message, "I got your email, Will. Please don't do this. I am concerned that you are contemplating suicide. I felt the same way after my travel. It is not the answer. Let me help you, as someone once helped me.. It is not your fault. You are not a violent man. You wouldn't have hurt her if you were in your right mind. Time travel has very serious effects on your mental and emotional well-being. You need to forgive yourself. She died in 1874, and nothing and no one can change that. It is not your fault. Please call me back."

A couple of hours later, he tried calling the hotel again to see if Will had returned. The desk clerk told him that Will had been found hanging outside his room. Dr. Oberton thanked the clerk and began to cry as he started to gather together all the information he had collected over the years about time travel.

He was going to burn it in a barrel in the backyard, just as he was going to sear it from his memory. Man is too egotistical... too sure of his ability to fix things... to be trusted with time travel now... or maybe ever.

# Did you enjoy this book?

Recommend it to a friend. And please consider **rating it and/or leaving a brief review** at Amazon, Barnes & Noble, and Goodreads.

# Sharon Marie Provost

## About the author

Sharon Marie Provost is the co-author with Stephen H. Provost of *Christmas Nightmare's Eve*, and her story "Shining Night" from that volume also appears in *The ACES Anthology 2023*. As chief operating officer of Dragon Crown Books Ltd., she served as the co-editor of the latter work, a project highlighting short stories and poetry from Northern Nevada writers. Sharon is a longtime resident of Carson City, where she lives with her husband and her pets. She worked for 20 years as a veterinary office manager and is the owner of champion of dog-trial poodles, and the creator of handmade dreamcatchers and chainmaille jewelry. You can find her at local craft fairs, author events, and at "Sharon's Dreams" on Facebook.

## Also by
# Sharon Marie Provost

*Christmas Nightmare's Eve* (with Stephen H. Provost)
*The ACES Anthology* (contributor)

Made in the USA
Middletown, DE
30 August 2025